Lucy was still co response when Lennox and remin Iain.'

He whistled. 'I'd forgotten that,' he said. 'Perhaps we should warn our new colleague to give that lady a wide berth.' He looked directly at Lucy. 'Ms Fearnan is a surgeon at the Northern General Hospital. She is also an ardent feminist of great volatility and bad temper,' he told her, with a curl of the lip that caused Lucy's large blue eyes to flash fire.

'As it happens, I've already heard of her,' she returned frostily. 'But my informant painted a very different picture.'

He raised an eyebrow. 'Really? I'm most surprised. But there, we all speak as we find, so your informant must have been lucky. If you are unfortunate enough to make Maggie Fearnan's acquaintance, I'd be willing to bet you end up agreeing with me.'

Over my dead body! thought Lucy fiercely, meeting Iain Lennox's compelling stare without smiling. After a long minute he said evenly, 'Don't let me keep you, Miss Trent.' He turned his back dismissively and swept out of the office. I can see what Ma means about him, Lucy thought. All the same, Mr Iain Lennox FRCS, you can look forward to more arguments if you persist in miscalling my mother in my hearing! She had completely forgotten promising Maggie to go canny.

Drusilla Douglas is a physiotherapist who has written numerous short stories—mainly for Scottish based magazines. Now the luxury of working part-time has provided her with the leisure necessary to embark on novels.

Previous Titles

A SERIOUS CASE OF CONFUSION
THE TROUBLE WITH DOCTORS
THE VALLERSAY CURE

# SURGEON'S DAUGHTER

BY

DRUSILLA DOUGLAS

MILLS & BOON LIMITED
ETON HOUSE    18–24 PARADISE ROAD
RICHMOND    SURREY    TW9 1SR

*First published in Great Britain 1991
by Mills & Boon Limited*

© Drusilla Douglas 1991

*Australian copyright 1991
Philippine copyright 1991
This edition 1991*

ISBN 0 263 77180 6

*Set in 10 on 11½ pt Linotron Plantin
03-9103-56485
Typeset in Great Britain by Centracet, Cambridge
Made and printed in Great Britain*

# CHAPTER ONE

Two candidates sat uneasily in their allotted chairs. When their eyes met, they exchanged brief smiles. There were three of them altogether and the first was already being grilled on the other side of that massive panelled door. The door opened and she came out, looking bewildered.

'Miss Gordon next, please,' requested the hospital manager's personal assistant from the doorway.

The second hopeful jumped up too quickly, dropping her bag. When that door eventually clicked shut behind her, Lucy asked the first girl how it had gone.

'I don't know. They were all so nice to me that I couldn't make out what they were thinking.' She gulped. 'I don't know how you can look so calm when you're last.'

Did she really? Lucy didn't feel all that calm. 'Having a surname beginning with T, I suppose I must have got used to it,' she returned wryly. Conversation lapsed.

The second girl was in longer—at least it seemed longer. But she emerged at last, and Lucy rose to her feet, smoothing the skirt of her cream poly-cotton shirt-waister, pushing back a wayward frond of her thick blue-black hair. She noticed that the second candidate was smiling. Did she know already that she had got the job? 'Miss Trent, please.' Lucy lifted her neat little chin another half-inch and followed the usher into the committee-room.

Two women and two men were sitting on the far side of a long table. When the man in the middle said, 'Please

5

sit down, Miss Trent,' Lucy sat. Then the man waved a
hand to his right. 'Dr Smith is a senior lecturer in
physiotherapy at Queen's College and Mrs Cumnock,
our superintendent physiotherapist, you have already
met.' He turned to his left to introduce, 'Mr Lennox,
consultant orthopaedic surgeon.'

The two women had smiled and said, 'Good afternoon,' but with just the merest nod of acknowledgement,
Mr Lennox returned to his rapid note-making. The
spokeman then introduced himself as the personal officer, Mr Selkirk.

'Thank you,' murmured Lucy, having smiled—with
composure, she hoped—all along the line.

Mr Selkirk wanted to know why Lucy wished to work
in Glasgow and whether she had ever been seriously ill.
Dr Smith was there to make sure that Lucy knew how
to guide the first tentative steps of any students seconded
for clinical experience, and Mrs Cumnock had already
asked her questions when she showed Lucy around the
physiotherapy department. So it was left to Mr Lennox
to conduct the lengthiest inquisition. After all, it was his
patients Lucy was being assessed as competent to treat.

So far, all she'd seen of him was the top of his bright
brown curly head, resting, as he wrote, on one strong,
well-kept hand. Now she found herself under steady
scrutiny from a pair of darkly tawny, green-flecked eyes.
Most unusual—and rather sexy. Lucy was aghast. What
a thought to be having at a time like this—and in spite
of knowing what she did about him too! She swallowed
hard and sat up a little straighter in her chair.

'Why Orthopaedics, Miss Trent?' he began in a deep
resonant voice.

'Because it's one of the specialities where a physiotherapist's contribution is particularly important.'

He didn't dispute that. 'And do you like to feel important?'

'I like to feel useful, sir.'

'You could be just as useful treating stroke patients, for example.'

'Yes, sir, but it was considered at St Crispin's that I had a—a particular facility for treating orthopaedic cases.'

'Perhaps that's why Professor Forde has given you such a glowing reference.' A weighty pause. 'But then again, there are other reasons for giving glowing references, are there not?'

Lucy would have known what he meant even without Mrs Cumnock's astonished gasp. 'Yes, sir—I have heard it said that that's one way of getting rid of undesirables,' she returned steadily. 'I just hope that wasn't the Professor's reason in my case.'

She knew quite well it wasn't, or why would he have given her that wonderful gold-plated pen and pencil set when she left? And that man knows it too, she discerned, noting the tiny upturn of Mr Lennox's mobile, well-cut mouth. He just wanted to find out if he could unsettle me.

Another calculated pause and then, 'I'm always interested to know why women choose hospital work, Miss Trent, when there are better paid, more glamorous and less stressful possibilities open to them.'

'Given that I have to earn my own living, I prefer to do it in a meaningful way—quite apart from family tradition. My father and grandfather are doctors, so I knew exactly what I was taking on.' Ma had said it would be better not to mention her, things being the way they were.

'So it would seem. Now let's find out if you know how to go about the job.' He proceeded to give Lucy a viva on treatments and anatomy the like of which she hadn't undergone since graduating—and certainly hadn't expected today. One or two of the questions she knew she could have answered more fully, given more time, but at least she made no mistakes. She had no idea just how keyed up she was until Mr Lennox turned at last to the personnel officer and said, 'I have no more questions for this candidate.' Lucy felt a tiny rush of relief then, and realised that her palms were sweating.

'Thank you for coming, Miss Trent. Would you wait outside, please?'

'Yes, Mr Selkirk. And thank you all for seeing me.'

'Well?' demanded the other girls in unison when Lucy returned to the waiting-room. 'You were certainly in there long enough!' added the first to be interviewed.

'I expect that was because they knew absolutely nothing about me, whereas you're both Glasgow trained.' And therefore with the edge on me, Lucy added to herself. She sat down and tried to look unconcerned, which wasn't easy after that grilling. The girl Gordon was still looking as if the outcome was a foregone conclusion. If it was, then why had that man Lennox given her such a rough passage? Perhaps he was a Scottish Nationalist who just didn't like the English! Unless he had known all the time whose daughter she was. . .!

The door opened. 'Miss Trent, would you go in, please?'

'M-me?'

'Yes, you, Miss Trent.' The PA was holding open the door.

Lucy re-entered the room to see that all the panel members were smiling—even the chief inquisitor. 'It is now my pleasant duty to offer you the post of senior orthopaedic physiotherapist here at the Glasgow General

Hospital, Miss Trent,' said the personnel officer. 'Do you accept?'

'Oh, yes—yes, I do! Thank you very much, Mr Selkirk. Thank you all very much.'

'Good. Would you be able to start at the beginning of next month?'

That was almost three weeks away, and Lucy had been hoping to start at once. But of course she said, 'Just whenever you wish, Mr Selkirk.'

Then Mr Lennox leaned forward and whispered something to the personnel officer, who answered doubtfully, 'I'm not at all sure that the Finance Department——'

Irritably, the consultant waved a silencing hand. 'Thanks to that unwarranted delay in advertising the post, it's already been vacant quite long enough to satisfy the fiercest passion for economy, so leave this to me, will you?' He turned his remarkable eyes on Lucy. 'You've already left your previous post, so if I can fix it, could you start next week?'

When Lucy answered that she'd be delighted, he said, 'Excellent. And would you also be willing to come to a ward round tomorrow morning, so as not to waste time on Monday?'

'Certainly, sir.'

'I'm quite sure we couldn't pay Miss Trent for tomorrow,' warned the PO.

'True professionals don't quibble about that sort of thing. They're more interested in doing what's best for their patients. Right, Miss Trent?'

'Right, sir.' If he had suggested working all weekend for nothing, Lucy would probably have agreed. He wasn't, she felt, the sort of man with whom it would be either easy or wise to disagree.

'Nine-thirty on the Orthopaedic Unit tomorrow morning, then.' Mr Lennox stood up and Lucy saw that he wasn't quite as tall as the breadth of his shoulders had suggested. Only five ten or eleven, perhaps. . . 'Good afternoon,' he said, encompassing them all. A final head-to-toe appraisal for Lucy and he was gone.

When the rest of the panel dispersed, Mrs Cumnock walked down to the car park with Lucy, alternately expressing the hope that Lucy would enjoy her new post and apologising for Mr Lennox's uncompromising attitude. 'If Mr Dunning, our senior orthopaedic consultant, hadn't been on holiday, he would have interviewed you,' she said. 'He's a much less—um—formidable character.'

Lucy only just managed not to say that she knew that and hurried instead to assure the superintendent that she quite understood Mr Lennox's anxiety to find out all about her. Except that he hadn't discovered the one thing that would probably have ensured his veto on her appointment!

Mrs Cumnock then revealed that, what with one thing and another, they were very short of staff and she was very sorry, but Lucy would have to manage single-handed for the time being.

Single-handed on a seventy-bedded acute unit? No wonder she had kept that piece of news a secret until I'd accepted, realised Lucy ruefully. 'Ah, well,' she said with a small sigh, 'as long as the surgeons are aware of the situation, I presume they'll not be expecting any miracles.'

They shook hands, exchanged goodbyes and parted. Lucy got into her brand new Nova, edged it out into the traffic and headed north. The rush hour was over by now, which was a relief. She knew Glasgow fairly well, but, not having driven much in the sprawling city, she needed all her concentration to avoid getting lost. Once clear of the north-west suburbs, however, and heading towards Loch Lomond on a pleasant country road, she found her thoughts returning to her interview. Thanks to that man Lennox, it must have been about the toughest that could have been devised. Ma had admitted to crossing swords with him more than once. It must have been an ordeal—even for her!

Lucy knew quite well that her mother had a reputation for ruthlessness and determination at work. But then she'd needed to be that way. This might be the age of equal opportunity, but the message had been slow getting through to the surgical profession—and for a woman to aspire to be an orthopaedic surgeon, of all things, was almost unprecedented. Over the years, and quite without self-pity, Ma had let slip quite a lot about her hard fight to get to the top.

And it wasn't only her professional life that had been difficult. As so often before, Lucy wondered again now just what it was that had attracted her totally dissimilar parents to one another. Whatever it was, it hadn't lasted, and they had divorced when she was three. Leaving Lucy in the capable and loving care of her own mother, Lucy's mother had returned to medicine, working long and hard to make up for the time lost to her disastrous marriage. But five years later, Gran had died and Father had resurfaced with the offer of a good boarding-school down in England, close to him. At first he had been the devoted parent, coming regularly at weekends and half-terms to shower Lucy with presents and treats. But once he'd remarried, the visits had got fewer, and by the time Lucy had a half-brother, they had ceased altogether, leaving her desolate in term-time and longing for her holidays in Scotland with her mother and grandfather. Older than her years, as the children of broken homes so often were, Lucy hid her father's neglect, sensing that her mother had troubles enough of her own.

Lucy had chosen to take her physio training in London

at St Crispin's Hospital, because her best school friend had. And she'd stayed on to work there afterwards on account of a rather nice young doctor. Then two months ago he had casually announced one day that he was getting married. Lucy was stunned. Where had she gone wrong, why had she never realised what was happening, and why had he never said? She'd stayed just long enough to work out her notice, then hurried North to Ma and Grandfather Jock.

Ma had been pleased, though she'd tried hard not to show it. 'This isn't such a bad idea of yours, Luce,' she had said offhandedly. 'Standards are as high in this city as anywhere, so you should enjoy your work. There is one thing, though. I'm not the most popular surgeon in Glasgow, so you'd better not let on that you're my daughter until you've landed a job and charmed all your colleagues into thinking you're indispensable. Now then, lassie, get your coat on. We're going out to buy you a decent car. It's a miracle you got here at all in that clapped-out old banger you're driving now!'

Lucy drove through the charming little town of Drymen, coming about fifteen minutes later to the pretty lochside cottage her grandfather had bought when he'd retired from general practice. Now that he was getting old, Ma made the cottage her home too, though she also had a small flat near her hospital for use when on call. Lucy would be using it too—at least to begin with.

She put away her car and went in by the back door. Netta, floury to the elbows, was standing at the kitchen table making pastry. Netta Jack had been with the family since Maggie was twelve and adored them all, as they adored her. She looked up, saw Lucy and demanded, 'Well?'

'I got it, Netta! Isn't it wonderful?' Lucy danced over to Netta and gave her a hug.

'Havers! I telt ye ye would, did I no'? Now for pity's sake away through to the front and tell the auld yin—he's been up an' doon like a ferret wi' piles this past hour!'

Lucy choked on a giggle and ran to find her grandfather, thinking that all those Southerners who thought the Scots were humourless should meet their Netta. Old Jock Fearnan had been reading his BMJ in the sun-lounge with its wonderful view of Loch Lomond. When he heard Lucy coming, he threw it aside and snatched off his spectacles. One look at his granddaughter's face was enough to tell him her news, but he barely had time to kiss and congratulate her before the back door crashed shut the way it always did when Maggie Fearnan entered the cottage. 'She'll have it all down about our ears one of these days,' he said resignedly as Maggie burst through the french windows, eyes alight.

'Netta told me!' She clapped her daughter vigorously on the back and planted a smacking kiss on her cheek. 'I knew you could do it, Luce. So how was it?'

'Ma, you were dead right about that man Lennox. He's a real tiger, and he grilled me as if he was interviewing me for a registrar's job—at least!'

'That figures, but he must have been satisfied, and that's the main thing. All the same, if he'd had any idea who you are. . .' Maggie whistled long and loud before greeting her father, then going back into the sitting-room to fetch them all a sherry.

That done, she dropped into a chair and lit the inevitable cigarette. Jock got up and pointedly opened another window, while Lucy said, 'I know you're always saying you're not very popular, Ma, but if there is something more, apropos Mr Lennox, then you'd better tell me—now that I've got to work with him.'

'He thinks I blighted his career,' returned Maggie with perfect calm.

Lucy blinked. 'I don't see how you possibly could have. After all, to be a consultant at—what? Thirty-six or -seven——'

'Iain Lennox is only thirty-four.' Maggie kicked off her shoes and put her feet up on the windowsill. 'And if he smiled more, then that's how old he'd look. He was on my team some years back. I found him to be very hard-working, very intelligent and shaping up to be a well-above-average surgeon. But he was in too much of a hurry. He wanted me to put him forward for a senior registrarship before he was ready—and I refused. He might have coped, but more likely he wouldn't have, and a promising career would have collapsed. It's entirely thanks to me that he's where he is today, though I doubt he'd ever admit it.'

'Now I understand,' said Lucy slowly.

'No, you do not, Luce!' Maggie denied hotly. 'If I'd been a *man*, he'd have accepted what I did and forgiven me long since. By now, we'd likely be the best of pals. But I'm a woman who's had the cheek to set herself up as a surgeon, and it's that he can't forgive me for—him and a muckle others!'

Old Jock had been shaking his head sadly while Maggie ranted on. 'They don't call you Battling Maggie Fearnan for nothing, my lass,' he said as soon as he got the chance. 'If you'd only calm down a bit—show them your softer side—things would be so much easier for you. A soft answer turneth away wrath, remember.'

Maggie let out a derisive hoot. 'Not in the circles I move in, it doesn't! Your average male surgeon is still a rabid chauvinist, Dad. Why else do so few women penetrate the citadel? Believe me, if I didn't rave and shout, nobody'd ever listen.' She stubbed out her half-smoked cigarette and got to her feet; tall, rangy, but surely immensely strong—or how could she cope so well with her job? 'Come on, Luce,' she urged. 'Help your poor downtrodden old ma to set the table. As it's such a beautiful evening, Netta thinks we should have supper out here and get the benefit of the sun.'

With supper over, the dishwasher fed, Netta away to watch television and Jock writing a letter, Maggie said, 'Come for a stroll by the loch, daughter.'

'Surely, but I'd better change my shoes first.' Lucy also collected a cardigan while upstairs. Even in June, it could be cool by the water at this time of day.

Maggie wanted to talk about Lucy's new job, and the minute they had shut the garden gate and started down the gravelled path to the shore, she said, 'Not to worry about Tom Dunning letting the cat out of the bag, Luce. I shall drop him a warning note at home before he starts work again after his holiday.'

'You're so thoughtful, Ma,' said Lucy. I hadn't even considered the possibility of that.'

Tom Dunning, a friend since student days, was one of the few male colleagues with whom Maggie was on intimate terms. He was, of course, also the senior orthopaedic surgeon at Glasgow General Hospital. 'Apart from Tom,' Maggie continued, 'I can't think of anybody else at the General who's likely to know of the connection.' She gave a mirthless laugh. 'I doubt if more than half a dozen folk in Glasgow even remember that Maggie Fearnan was once briefly married—or that she ever did anything so normal as conceive and give birth! It's lucky for you, my child, that you went away to your posh English school at such an early age and collected that

Southern accent. Nobody would ever connect you with foul-mouthed, feminist old Mag!'

Lucy stopped walking and faced her mother. 'Stop putting yourself down, Ma. I won't have it. You don't swear—well, not much—you're certainly no feminist, and fifty is not old. Anyway, supposing they do find out you're my mother? I'm very proud of you and all you've achieved. And so I'll bloody well tell 'em!'

'Look like you're doing now and use that sort of language, and nobody'll be in any doubt. All right, so you're cock-a-hoop because you've landed a nice job. But that's only the start. Promise me you'll go canny, Luce. Please!'

Lucy simmered down. Much as she resented the reputation heaped on her mother, she knew that Maggie was right. She had to live in the world as it was, and it was only common sense to go canny. 'I promise, Ma—I promise. I'm going to be as diplomatic and as—as well behaved as I know how.'

'That's my girl!' Maggie embraced and kissed her daughter with a tenderness that, had they seen it, would have sent her opponents at the Royal College of Surgeons rushing off to the nearest opticians for new glasses. 'We'll only go as far as the Point,' she decided. 'You must get an early night and be sparkling fresh and eager for that ward round tomorrow.'

Mr Lennox had said nine-thirty, and ten minutes before that Lucy pushed open the swing doors and stepped into the main corridor of Orthopaedics. She had taken great pains to be absolutely immaculate. New white tunic and navy trousers above highly polished navy shoes. Blue-black hair washed that morning and secured at the back with a navy petersham bow. A discreet minimum of make-up carefully applied. Thickly lashed, smoky-blue eyes sparkling with anticipation. On the way here a passing porter had endorsed her satisfactory appearance with a long low whistle.

The wide corridor seemed endless, with countless doors on either side. So which one concealed the assembling ward team?

'Mr Lennox?' echoed the earnest-looking staff nurse Lucy appealed to. 'Well now, our glamorous lady houseman is in the dotctors' room, so it's a safe bet that he's in there too. Third door on the left—you can't miss it.'

'Thank you very much, Staff,' returned Lucy in her clear English voice, realising as she hurried along that she'd learned rather more about the man than just his whereabouts. She fetched up by the open door and stood there, waiting to be noticed.

A white-coated Iain Lennox was perched casually on the windowsill, arms folded and long legs outstretched. His amazing eyes were alight with amusement as he surveyed the slim blonde standing with her back half turned to the door. Lucy found it hard to believe that this animated, attractive-looking man was the one who had given her such a hard time the day before. 'No, I'm not a chauvinist,' he was insisting in his deep voice. 'I'm merely being practical when I say that orthopaedic surgery is not a suitable speciality for a woman. It requires far more strength and stamina than any normal woman can muster. You must be out of your mind to consider it, Lois.'

'Ms Fearnan of the Northern General Hospital manages all right.'

Lucy didn't miss the scornful twist of his handsome mouth as he retorted swiftly, 'I said any *normal* woman. Maggie Fearnan is without doubt a direct descendant of Attila the Hun—and I speak with all the authority of one who suffered for six long months as her registrar.'

Lucy felt her quick temper rising, and she was grateful when the girl retorted quickly, 'You may not like her, Iain, but you've got to admit that she's a damn fine surgeon.'

'I'm always prepared to admit an obvious truth,' he answered with a pious magnanimity that had Lucy clenching her fists. 'But look at the cost. She's made a lot of enemies and sacrificed any femininity she ever possessed. You wouldn't want that to happen to you, would you?'

To Lucy's utter consternation, the smile he bent on Lois as he asked that left *her* feeling quite lightheaded. Heaven only knew what it had done to its rightful recipient! She waited for the girl to make some equally flirtatious response, but a loud rumbling further down the corridor took her attention. Lucy stepped back out of sight as a middle-aged but serenely beautiful white-haired sister brought a heavy trolley of case notes and X-rays to a halt at the door. 'Nine-thirty, Mr Lennox,' she said calmly and firmly.

He still hadn't spotted Lucy, and he came to the door, frowning. 'The new physiotherapist was appointed yesterday and undertook to be here for the round. Ah well, I suppose we'll just have to——'

Lucy stepped forward out of the shadow. 'Good morning, sir,' she said quietly.

The frown didn't lessen all that much. 'It would have been nice if you'd been earlier, Miss Trent. There are one or two things I wanted to say to you first.'

'I was early, sir, but when I asked where you were, I was told that you were in—er—consultation with your house officer. I didn't think you'd want me to interrupt.' I'm not battling Maggie's daughter for nothing, she was thinking fiercely.

He was speechless for the moment; not something that

happened often, judging by the look of astonishment on the blonde's face and the dawning interest on Sister's. 'That was very considerate of you,' he allowed at last. 'Now let me introduce two of your new colleagues. Sister Clyde, undisputed head of the unit. Dr Baird, house officer.' Murmured greetings having been exchanged, he asked, 'Where's the registrar, Sister?'

'Dr Carswell was called down to A and E a few minutes ago, sir.'

'And Mr Murray?'

'He's coming now.' Sister Clyde nodded towards a stocky, good-humoured-looking man, pounding down the corridor at a run.

The consultant introduced him to Lucy before asking, 'Is there a problem, Charles?'

'Old Mrs Barr on Geriatrics. She's fallen out of bed again, having climbed right over the safety rail, would you believe? And this time I'm pretty sure she's got herself a hip fracture. I told them we'd try to operate some time today if the X-rays are positive.'

'By the sound of it, it'll be a miracle if they're not.' He looked at Sister and asked, 'Do we have a bed? She really ought to come to us straight from Theatre—that ward isn't constructed for keeping a close watch on post-op patients.'

'I'm afraid not, Mr Lennox, unless you can discharge somebody on the round.'

Lucy stood quietly by thinking that if she closed her eyes she could imagine herself back at St Crispin's, where a conversation very like this would be going on right now as Professor Forde embarked on his weekly round.

They began in the men's ward, and the first patient was a lad of eighteen or so, with spiky hair, earrings and heavily tattooed forearms. His right leg was on traction in a Thomas splint and the thigh was heavily bandaged.

'Good morning, Kevin,' said Mr Lennox briskly. 'How goes it, then?'

'Too bluidy slow,' returned the boy sulkily.

Mr Lennox replied impassively that that, unfortunately, was the way it went. 'No prizes for guessing this patient's injury, Miss Trent,' he added as he took the X-ray Charles Murray had ready for him.

He held it up to the light, and as Lois Baird seemed more interested in examining her nails than in looking at the film, Lucy sidled round her to peer at it under Mr Lennox's uplifted arm. The reward for her zeal was a clout on the head from his elbow when he swung round. 'Good grief! I really am sorry about that,' he said, sounding quite concerned. 'Apart from stars, did you see all you wanted?'

'Yes, thank you, sir.' As his expression was clearly inviting her to continue, Lucy reeled off, 'A compound, comminuted fracture, midshaft of femur—now showing good callus formation.'

'Well observed, but how do you know it was compound?'

Lucy bit her lip. 'I—I assumed it must have been, with all that fragmentation. . .'

'Don't look so uncertain; your assumption was quite correct.' He turned back to the patient. 'Things are going better than we expected, lad. Even so, we can't hurry Nature.'

'Why could ye no' ha'e nailed it togither like ye did his'n?' The boy pointed across the ward to a middle-aged man busily reading the *Sun*. 'He on'y came in last week and he's getting aboot on crutches.'

'You may both have broken the same bone, but the fractures were totally different—and so, therefore, is the treatment.'

'I jest hope ye ken what ye're at, that's a',' growled the boy truculently, earning himself a look from Sister that promised him a right good telling-off after the round.

Iain Lennox folded his arms across his broad chest and looked at the boy until Kevin looked away, embarrassed. Then the consultant said quietly, 'So do I, Mr McVeagh, so do I.' His tactics were far more effective than any angry retort would have been, and as they moved on to the next patient, Lucy felt the first faint dawning of respect.

Here was another fractured shaft of femur, and yet another in the third bed. Nothing to choose between these two, realised Lucy, writing busily in her notebook. And all three would be in her daily maintenance class. That first patient, Kevin McVeagh, could well be a problem. Would she cope with him as well as Mr Lennox had?

On to Mr Govan next. He had been unfortunate enough to fracture both calcaneum bones at the same time. 'How are the calcanei usually fractured, Miss Trent?' asked the consultant.

'By falling and landing heavily on the heels, sir.'

'Any possible complications if the fall is from a considerable height?'

'Vertebral fractures—or even a fracture of the occipital bone, sir.'

Iain Lennox nodded approvingly. 'And what are you going to do for this man?'

Lucy looked again at his grossly swollen feet propped up in elevation. 'Ice packs and ultra-sound to disperse the swelling before it thickens, sir. But avoiding the fracture sites, of course. I mustn't disrupt the healing process.'

'I was very relieved to hear that proviso, Miss Trent,'

was the humorous reply, accompanied by almost as good a smile as the one he had bestowed earlier on Lois Baird.

Moving on, Lucy was amused to hear her whisper to Charles Murray, 'If he's going to bother with that wretched physio all the way round, we'll be here all morning!'

'Steady, dear, your green eyes are showing,' the senior registrar whispered back. What a good thing Mr Lennox happened to be conferring with Sister at that moment!

The next patient was suffering from that perennial headache for physios, a VSK, short for a very stiff knee. Only just out of plaster, by the look of it; all swollen, misshapen, shiny and hard. Mr Lennox only managed to bend it about five miserable degrees. Having completed his examination, he spoke to Lucy again. 'Mr Watson was injured at his work in the shipyard eighteen weeks ago. He fractured all four condyles, femoral and tibial. We've done our bit, Miss Trent, so it's up to you now.'

'Thank you, sir.' Lucy accompanied that with a rueful look which he answered with a faint smile. Then she turned to the patient. 'You and I are going to be very, very busy for quite a while, Mr Watson.'

'Just so long as ye get me oot o' here before Hogmanay, hen,' he responded with typical Glasgow humour.

'If I don't, then I'll be right in line for the dole queue,' returned Lucy, earning herself smiles from all the team, except Lois Baird. Don't you be getting above yourself, seemed to be her message. Lucy wondered at her hostility. What was she afraid of?

The round continued. Iain Lennox seemed to carry every detail of the patients in his head and referred only occasionally to the notes. Quite a feat of memory, that. Lucy was also very impressed by the standard of surgery and patient care. That boy they'd just discharged, in particular. What a splendid piece of reconstruction Mr Lennox had done on that shattered foot, she readily admitted to herself as they walked in convoy down the corridor to the women's ward.

It was a different picture here, where most of the patients were old ladies with fractures resulting from quite trivial injuries. There were a few youngsters, though, such as Kevin's girlfriend Trisha, who had been riding pillion and was injured in the same crash. 'You'll have seen the Oxford brace before,' said Mr Lennox to Lucy, having giving some of the screws an extra turn or two after referring to the latest film of Trisha's badly damaged tibia.

'Yes, sir.'

'What's your opinion of it?'

She hadn't expected that. 'We-ell, being able to get early mobility of knee and ankle is certainly a help from my point of view,' she offered tactfully. But most of the patients disliked the thing, preferring to rest comparatively easily in plaster. This girl was no exception, judging by her expression.

Mr Lennox had noticed it too and he said, 'As I explained in the beginning, lassie, a few weeks of increased discomfort now will mean a better result and a quicker recovery overall. Now that can't be bad, can it?'

Trisha's resistance melted away under all that charm. 'I guess not, Mr Lennox,' she agreed, dimpling.

He seemed to be just as effective with the old ladies, and one bright-eyed old dear even pulled him down to be kissed when he told her she was now well enough to go home. The agile Mrs Barr from Geriatrics would be getting her bed here after all.

'I hope you found all that helpful, Miss Trent,' said

Mr Lennox confidently, falling into step beside Lucy for the return trip to Sister's office.

'It certainly was, sir. I can't guarantee to remember every detail offhand, but I know I'll feel the benefit when I treat the patients on—on. . . When *am* I to start work, sir?'

'On Monday, of course.' He seemed amazed that she should have doubted his ability to get his own way in the matter.

'Thank you, sir. And I'm looking forward to it,' Lucy added politely. It should have been an undiluted pleasure to know she would be working with so able a surgeon, but she couldn't quite forget that this man was one of her mother's denigrators.

Perhaps there had been some reservation apparent in her tone, because Iain Lennox returned quietly, 'I certainly hope so, Miss Trent,' as he gestured for her to precede him into the office.

Sister Clyde set about dispensing coffee with speed and efficiency, while Mr Murray made a phone call and Dr Baird cornered Mr Lennox to besiege him with a lot of questions so elementary as to betray her intention of keeping his attention for herself. So it fell to Sister to converse with the new girl, once everybody was served.

She began by asking Lucy if she had managed to find somewhere suitable to stay.

Lucy thanked her and said yes, thinking it best not to be too specific in case somebody connected Kelvindale Court with Maggie and brought her into the conversation. Yet not to expand a bit could sound unfriendly. 'It's not very near the hospital, unfortunately, but it's a lovely flat.'

'Which is perhaps more important.' Sister paused, feeling her way. 'Perhaps you have friends—or some family up here, Miss Trent.' Seeing Lucy's wary expression, she added, 'I was just wondering why you'd chosen Glasgow, dear.'

Lucy relaxed and cautiously admitted to an uncle, some aunts and a few scattered cousins. 'But I chose Glasgow because of its high reputation, Sister.' That came out pat, being exactly what Lucy had told the interviewing panel the previous day. They continued to chat on general matters for a few minutes more, but, when Mr Murray got up to leave, Lucy decided it was probably time to take her leave too. She stood up, catching the consultant's eye. 'If there's nothing else, Mr Lennox. . .'

'Not just now, but thank you very much for coming this morning. I'm sure we all look forward to seeing you back on Monday morning.'

'Monday, is it?' echoed Sister. 'I shall be off then, so perhaps you'd give me your address and phone number now, Miss Trent. Just a notion of Mr Dunning's—our senior consultant,' she explained, puzzled by Lucy's look of horror. 'If any member of the team needs to contact another urgently, it's so much quicker to do so directly than to go through the switchboard.'

And a jolly good notion too, Tom, old dear, thought Lucy—in any other circumstances! Still, Ma was ex-directory, so maybe nobody would make the connection. Quietly and for Sister's ears only, she recited the address and telephone number of her mother's little flat.

Trust the hostile Lois to overhear. 'Kelvindale Court? But that's that pricey block near the Northern General,' she exclaimed. 'You must be pretty well off for a physio, if you can afford to live there. At least two of the Northern's consultants do.'

'Really?' Lucy hoped she was looking suitably detached. 'Not having moved in yet, I've not met any of the neighbours.'

She was still congratulating herself on her well-turned response when Dr Baird turned wide eyes on Iain Lennox and reminded him, 'Maggie Fearnan lives there, Iain.'

He whistled. 'I'd forgotten that,' he said. 'Perhaps we should warn our new colleague to give that lady a wide berth.' He looked directly at Lucy. 'Ms Fearnan is a surgeon at the Northern General Hospital. She is also an ardent feminist of great volatility and bad temper,' he told her, with a curl of the lip that caused Lucy's large blue eyes to flash fire.

'As it happens, I've already heard of her,' she returned frostily. 'But my informant painted a very different picture.'

He raised an eyebrow. 'Really? I'm most surprised. But there, we all speak as we find, so your informant must have been lucky.' He gave Lucy that special smile of his, and this time it only served to fuel her anger. 'If you're unfortunate enough to make Maggie Fearnan's acquaintance, I'd be willing to bet you'll end up agreeing with me.'

Over my dead body! thought Lucy fiercely, meeting Iain Lennox's compelling stare without smiling. After a long minute he said evenly, 'Don't let me keep you, Miss Trent. Be here at eight-thirty sharp on Monday, if you please.' He turned his back dismissively. 'Thanks for the coffee, Sister.' Then he swept out of the office with Lois Baird pattering after him.

Lucy also thanked Sister before following slowly after them. I can see what Ma means about him, she thought. And he doesn't like to be contradicted, that's for sure. All the same, Mr Iain Lennox FRCS, you can look forward to more of the same if you persist in miscalling my mother in my hearing!

She had completely forgotten promising Maggie to go canny.

# CHAPTER TWO

LUCY soon discovered that there was no need to set the alarm on the nights that Maggie stayed in the flat. Maggie rose well before seven and crashed around from the word go, the way she always did. Awakened this morning by the banging of the bathroom door, Lucy turned on to her back and stared at the ceiling. The first day of my second week, she realised, and here's hoping it'll be easier than the first.

After that unfortunate disagreement with Mrs Cumnock last Friday, the superintendent had said she would really have to see what could be done about part-time help on Orthopaedics. But as she had gone on to mutter about Peter having to be robbed to pay Paul, Lucy had decided not to count on it.

'Bathroom's free, Luce,' trumpeted Maggie in passing.

'Thanks, Ma.' Lucy rolled out of bed and down the corridor to the shower. Yes, last week had been a killer. The only way she had coped even halfway with her formidable case load was to go in very early, leave equally late, take no more than twenty minutes for lunch and miss out coffee breaks altogether. The only member of the orthopaedic staff who seemed to work longer hours than she did was Mr Lennox—and he did at least get to sit down during a clinic!

Being sent for by the superintendent physio in the middle of the ward round last Friday was the last straw.

Lucy switched off the shower and reached for her towel. She was prepared to concede that Mrs Cumnock might have a point about wanting to see every physio at least once a day, but in that case—as Ma had said so emphatically when told—it was bloody well up to her to see that they all had the time in which to be seen! Lucy had kept her temper and explained how she had been arranging her day, and why. What had really got her dander up was discovering later on that Mrs Cumnock was checking up on her.

An impish smile broke over her face as she recalled Iain Lennox's response to that. She had overheard by pure chance while helping a patient down the corridor. 'None whatever. Of the highest professional calibre, I would say,' floated clearly out of the doctors' room in his resonant tones.

Somebody's getting a good character, she had thought, never dreaming. But after a short pause she heard him say, 'It's clear to me, Mrs Cumnock, that you're quite unaware of the heavy case load on this unit, so I think I should put you in the picture.' Only an angel could have resisted listening after that, and Lucy was the first to admit that she was no angel. There followed a masterly catalogue; he had missed nothing she had done over and above the call of duty that week. Lucy had known she was under surveillance, but had had no idea just how thorough it had been.

It was just after that telephone conversation that Mrs Cumnock appeared on the unit and told Lucy she was hoping to arrange some help.

'Luce! Your breakfast's ready and I'm off now.'

'Thanks, Ma. Bye, then—and see you tomorrow.' Maggie, having been on call all weekend, would be going home to the cottage that night. 'Love to Jock and Netta,' Lucy added a second too late as the outer door crashed shut behind her mother.

\* \* \*

When Lucy walked into the ward office that morning, the same staff nurse who had told her where to find Mr Lennox that first morning was sitting at Sister's desk and frowning at the Kardex. She looked up when Lucy said, 'Good morning, Staff. I was wondering if there were any weekend developments I ought to know about.'

'I suppose you mean like chests and things.'

What else? thought Lucy, nodding.

'Well, there's Mrs Dorward, the inter-trochanteric femoral fracture who was pinned and plated on Friday afternoon; she's chesty. Confused too. Then there's Mr Aitken and Mr Dodson. And you might like to have a go at Mrs Fraser too. How's that?'

'Wonderful. Any more bad chests?'

'Not than I can think of,' said Staff.

'Any emergency weekend admissions, then?'

'There were a couple yesterday. I know you're supposed to be treating them, but you'll need to talk to a doctor first.' Staff leaned across the desk and admitted in a rush, 'This is the first time I've been left in sole charge, and I'm not enjoying it.'

'You poor dear!' Lucy was very sorry now that she'd been a bit satirical with the girl, but before she could apologise there was a sharp buzzing somewhere close.

'Oh, lord, there's that emergency loo buzzer again. . .' Staff scrambled up, knocking things off the desk, as she ran out of the office.

Lucy picked up a fallen stapler and some papers before crossing over to the trolley to look at the chest X-rays of the patients Staff Nurse had mentioned. Then she found the post-op film of Mrs Dorward's hip. 'Looks good,' she muttered when she'd got it up on the viewing screen. 'Nice position, right length of plate——'

'Thank you very much. I'm so relieved,' said Mr Lennox gravely, just behind her.

Lucy flashed round, scarlet and gulping. 'Oh, dear—I'm sorry, sir. Just thinking aloud——' She calmed down on realising that he wasn't angry, but was in fact rather amused.

'Please don't apologise for paying me a compliment,' he said.

'You're—very kind, sir. All the same, I shouldn't have said that aloud.' Lucy swallowed again. This was surely the moment for it. . .' There's something else, sir. I meant what I said on my first day—about Mag—Ms Fearnan, but I didn't have to say it quite so—so forcefully. It wasn't polite. I'm sorry.' So how about that for diplomacy, then?

He was regarding her with open admiration now. 'You impressed me very much at interview as being honest, intelligent and extremely well informed,' he said slowly. 'But a woman who can also admit she may not always get it right? Miss Trent, you're a real find. Now, have you time to come and see yesterday's emergency admissions with me? They both need your attention.'

'Yes, sir—of course.'

Iain Lennox slipped smoothly into the higher gear he seemed to reserve for these occasions. 'Both are young men, both were involved in road traffic accidents and both have fractured ribs which initially will be your main concern. However, Calum Sinclair also sustained a dislocated hip—now reduced and immobilised—while Bill McInnes has several pelvic fractures. His symphysis pubis was disrupted, so we had to wire it. All things considered, it's a miracle that the urinary tract is intact.'

This speech had brought them to the male ward, where Mr Lennox left nothing to chance in either case. Having listened to both chests and outlined the affected areas with a skin pencil, he told the patients exactly what Lucy would be doing to them, and why.

'Thank you very much, sir,' she said with genuine gratitude—and no thought of currying favour this time. 'It's often so hard to make patients understand that one must hurt them a bit for their own good.'

'Which is exactly why I explained,' he returned matter-of-factly. 'But their discomfort should be minimal, as they've both had a shot of pethidine. I'd like them treated two-hourly, so Staff has instructions to administer more at appropriate intervals. No questions? Right! I'm off to clinic now, then.' He strode away as purposefully as he had come, and Lucy turned back to Calum Sinclair.

'Ready, then?' she asked gently.

'I never thought—the day would come when—a pretty girl—would urge me to—cough and spit,' he managed jerkily when Lucy was settling him down again after his treatment.

'Better out than in,' she returned brightly.

'Now me—I always tell Trish the opposite,' Kevin McVeagh called across the ward. I'll bet you do, thought Lucy, while pretending she hadn't heard. His meaning was unmistakable—his cronies were sniggering—and clearly Kevin had hoped to raise a blush.

'Keep up the deep breathing, Mr Sinclair,' instructed Lucy serenely, 'and I'll come back to see you again before lunch. Now then, Mr McInnes; your turn next. . .'

Both men were fully co-operative, which was more than could be said of Lucy's next customer, Mr Aitken. 'Cough? Ah niver cough, hen. It hurts ma bad leg.'

'Then it's no wonder you've got a clogged-up chest, Mr Aitken,' she said severely.

'Wha says?'

'I saw that on your X-ray.'

'Niver had no X-ray. Not on nothin,' he insisted stolidly.

'Just you leave him to me, hen,' advised the patient in the next bed. 'Ah'll give him a ciggie when ye're away—he'll cough soon enough then.'

'That's very helpful of you, Mr Johnstone, but perhaps I'd better have one more try. . .'

Mr Dodson was the exact opposite. He couldn't try hard enough. Would Sister consider putting them in adjacent beds? wondered Lucy. And would Mr Aitken respond to such a good example?

Nearly time to take the men's maintenance class, but she really ought to dash down the corridor and see to those chesty old ladies first. . .

Back in the men's ward, Kevin McVeagh treated Lucy to an undressing look before telling her, 'You're sure a nice-looking armful, hen.'

'Any more of that and I'll tell Trisha you're making up to other women behind her back.'

Before Kevin could answer that, Mike Craig, his next-bed neighbour, said, 'You're English, are you not? So what are you doing here? Could ye no' get a job in your own country?'

'Ah'm only half a Sassenach. Ma mither's a Paisley buddy and ma hairt's in the Hielans,' retorted Lucy in passable Glaswegian.

That earned her a roar of approval from all of them. 'Right, now we've had our fun, let's get down to some work,' she suggested when the laughter had died away.

A quick tour of the ward first, to remind each patient what he must not attempt, then straight into the exercise regime designed to keep up the muscle tone of those confined to bed. There was, of course, the usual back-chat. 'When did you get oot the Army, Sergeant?' demanded Mike Craig after Lucy had reminded him briskly that she'd said nice straight knees, please, when lifting uninjured legs off the bed.

'Whenever they sent for me to come and deal with you lot. Come on now, Mr Wilkie—that's only a three-pound weight you've got there. A wee lassie could lift that and no bother.'

'Then let's see you do it,' was the inevitable invitation.

'I would if it'd help your muscles, but I don't think it would, do you?'

Half an hour later, with the class completed and the wisecrackers claiming to be having heart attacks after all that drill, Lucy started on the individual treatments for specific problems.

First, the ice and ultra-sound for Mr Govan's grossly swollen feet. 'One fractured calcaneum would have been bad enough, but two busted heels in one go is rotten luck,' she sympathised.

'Aye, right enough, lass. But it was the bluidy ladder breakin' under us, ken—and me no' exactly a fly-weight.'

'Better to land on your feet than your head, though, Mr Govan. Make sure you get a really good ladder before you go back to work, won't you?' He was a self-employed window cleaner.

'Dinna fret, hen. I'll be looking for something a muckle bit nearer the ground when I get oot o' here, Ah'm telling ye!'

Next came twenty minutes of hard work with Mr Watson and his very stiff knee. Then firm re-bandaging of Mr Buchan's amputation stump which must be moulded into a better shape than this if it was to fit comfortably into his artificial limb. 'I'd like you to lie flat on your stomach until lunchtime, if you can bear it,' Lucy said afterwards. 'It would never do to get a permanent crick in that hip joint.'

She was giving exercises to Mr Scott, the sprightly eighty-year-old who had received a total hip replacement the week before, when wise-guy Kevin called out, 'Hiya, Barbie Doll!'

Lucy looked up to see Lois Baird teetering down the ward on her five-inch heels. She grinned discreetly. Having insulted the consultant on a ward round, Kevin hadn't hesitated to do the same for the houseman.

Lois came up and said, 'Find something else to do, would you, Miss Trent? I need to take a blood sample from this man.'

Lucy blinked, less at the request than at the way it was made. 'Certainly, Dr Baird,' she agreed with exaggerated courtesy. Let her see that *some* people knew how to behave! She didn't have to anguish over how to fill in the time; Mr Aitken had done next to nothing in the morning class.

'Biscuit crumbs,' whispered the helpful Mr Johnstone in the next bed when Lucy had failed once again.

'I beg your pardon?' she returned, totally at sea.

'There's nothing like a muckle of gey great crumbs in the bed to get 'em moving, hen. Though mebbe dried peas'd be better,' he added thoughtfully.

His methods might be unorthodox, but Lucy could see how effective they could prove. 'Have you ever thought of taking up physiotherapy, Mr Johnstone?' she asked with a smile.

'Aye, Ah did, as a matter of fact, only the money's better down at the docks.'

'I wish I had time to stand talking to the patients,' observed Lois Baird acidly in passing. 'Mr Scott is waiting for you,' she added reprovingly over her shoulder.

'Take nae notice, hen,' recommended Mr Johnstone. 'Yon's a lassie who'd stand a' day talking to the doctors if they'd let her. She's jest worried aboot the competition a bonny wee soul like yourself could be.'

Patients missed nothing. Why would they, when they'd nothing else to do all day but watch the staff?

With Mr Scott's exercises completed and him escorted to the day-room, it was time to treat the chests again. Oh, no! Surely that wasn't the lunch trolley rumbling down the corridor already?

Chest treatments couldn't be rushed, and Lucy's lunch hour was half over before she thought of looking at her watch. Just about time to dash down to the canteen for a sandwich. She had made her selection and arrived at the cash-out before she realised she hadn't got her purse. 'I suppose you couldn't trust me?' she asked hopefully of the girl behind the till.

'Sorry, hen, but's that's more than my life's worth.' She pointed to the large notice overhead, proclaiming Positively No Credit. 'Can you no' see anybody you know?'

'I shouldn't think so—I've only been here a week,' returned Lucy, looking round despairingly. She spotted Mr Lennox in conversation with a distinguished-looking man who had to be a consultant and quickly averted her eyes. 'Sorry—I shall just have to put these back.'

The girl was looking so sorry for her. 'Look, I'll just— oh, thanks, Doctor. That'll be one twenty-five. See, you'll not be starving after all,' she said as she counted change into an outstretched hand that was scrupulously clean and attached to a tanned wrist encircled by an expensive but plain gold watch. Above that, an inch or two of spotless shirt cuff protruded from a starched white coat sleeve.

Lucy transferred her gaze to the smiling face of her benefactor, although she had already guessed his identity. 'You shouldn't have—didn't need. . .' What had happened to her voice, never mind her manners!

Iain Lennox took Lucy's tray with one hand and her elbow with the other, drawing her aside. 'Somebody had to—you were causing quite a hold-up.'

'You're very kind. All the same——' Lucy found herself thrust into a chair with her lunch on the table in front of her.

'Take your time over that modest meal, Miss Trent. You may have a heavy work load, but getting dyspepsia'll not help,' he advised before leaving with the other man, who had been watching the exchange with interest.

Old ladies couldn't be hurried. They also had a higher than average need for trips to the toilet during treatment. By the time Lucy had tucked up the tenth of them it was getting on for six o'clock. She stretched her weary arms, prompting her patient to sympathise, 'You'll have had a long day, dear.'

'Long enough, but it's over now—and what a nice way to end it. You're a model patient, Mrs Moffat.' Whereupon the patient preened with pleasure and they parted with mutual esteem.

The promised help had not materialised, and Lucy was shaking her head ruefully as she made for the stairs. She hadn't wasted a moment that day, but, just as last week, too many of her treatments had been shorter than she would have liked.

'You're looking gey trachled, Miss Trent,' observed a man's voice, and Lucy came out of her troubled thoughts to see the senior registrar smiling kindly on her.

'The usual story, Mr Murray. Too much to do and too short a day.'

'You seem to stretch yours, though. Are you girls not supposed to finish at five, on account of your work being so physically demanding?'

'On paper, yes, but in practice. . .' Lucy shook her

head again. 'Am I right in assuming that the two men with fractured ribs should be treated again this evening?'

'Absolutely, but don't tell me you're on tonight as well!'

'No, thank goodness. Just wanted to be sure before putting them on the list.'

'Good lass! See you tomorrow, then.'

'Yes—goodbye, Mr Murray.'

After lunch, Lucy had returned to the unit via Physiotherapy to pick up her purse and be ready to pay Mr Lennox what she owed next time she saw him. When she did spot him, though, he had been smiling down on Lois Baird again and probably wouldn't welcome the interruption. Now, rather than be thought dilatory in settling her debts, she made a detour through Outpatients and left the money with a note of thanks on his consulting-room desk. That done, she ran into Charles Murray again.

'Oh, good,' he said, 'because after I saw you, I had an idea. Are you doing anything tonight?'

You don't waste much time, thought Lucy, even as he went on to explain, 'Lois has been trying all day to swap tonight's duties with another houseman, but no dice, which leaves us one short for the skittles team. I suppose you couldn't deputise, could you? I'd buy you a pint.'

'Make that a half and I'll find myself unable to refuse,' responded Lucy. She might be tired, but this would be a good chance to get to know some of her new colleagues a bit better.

'Bless you for an angel! See you in the pub across the road at eight.' He paused. 'We're playing those aces from Paediatrics tonight—I hope you're good.'

'Mr Murray, you're looking at the ex-captain of St Crispin's all-conquering team.'

'Now I know why you got the job,' he returned

teasingly. 'So eight at the Jacobite Tavern, then. See you!'

It was hardly worth going home and back, so Lucy settled for a shower in Physio and a bar supper at the pub.

'Skittles Alley?' repeated the barman when Lucy asked him after paying her bill. 'Round the back and across the car park, hen.'

The place had obviously been converted from stables, judging by the sloping, raftered roof and all the hooks and nails protruding from the rough whitewashed walls. Apart from the alley, there was enough space for a few benches and tables, as well as a small bar in one corner.

Lucy was astonished enough to see earnest Staff Nurse Munro propping up the bar in a vivid green tracksuit, but what really stopped her in her tracks was the sight of Iain Lennox. He had his back to her, but there was no mistaking that bright brown curly hair and those shoulders, enhanced as they were by a casual, tweedy-looking sweater. A *consultant*? On a *skittles* team? Just as he turned round to see who the man he was talking to was staring at, Lucy remembered Ma telling her that his elevation to the hospital peerage was very recent.

The way he said, 'Good lord!' was hardly flattering. But the expression on his face undoubtedly was, as he took in her flowing dark hair released from its daytime bondage and her slim but very feminine outline in the dusky pink jersey blouse and navy uniform trousers, comprising the most suitable outfit she could manage at such short notice. Charles Murray hadn't arrived, so Lucy explained that he had engaged her as substitute for Dr Baird.

While Mr Lennox was recovering from his surprise, his companion stepped forward and said, 'I'm David

Drimmon, the senior paediatric registrar. And you are. . .?'

'Miss Trent is our new physiotherapist,' said Iain Lennox in a warning sort of voice. Why? Lucy was thinking that David Drimmon looked rather nice.

'Why is it that Ortho always attracts the beauties?' Dr Drimmon wondered, fingering Lucy's upper arm and staring deep into her eyes.

Hastily she revised her original assessment and marked him down as over-eager for the kill. 'You're awfully kind, Doctor,' she remarked with apparent simplicity, before calling over to Staff, 'Did you hear that, Essie? Dr Drimmon is paying us compliments.'

He removed his hand, unsure whether that had been guilelessness or sophistication on Lucy's part.

Iain Lennox was in no such doubt. His tawny eyes sparkled with amusement as he drew Lucy towards the bar before David could. 'What'll you drink?'

'Lime juice and ginger beer, please, sir.'

'Why? Are you on call too?'

'No—I just like that. Are you on call, then, sir?'

He placed Lucy's order before explaining, 'Every blessed night until Mr Dunning comes back on Friday. But Charles is actually first on tonight. He's over in A and E at the moment.' He handed Lucy her drink.

She thanked him before saying, 'By the way, sir, I put the money I owed you for my lunch on your desk.'

'I know—I found it. That was very prompt of you.'

'Not at all—I was very grateful, sir.'

He finished his tonic water and put the glass down on the bar with a thump. 'D'you think you could drop this "sir" business?' he asked plaintively. 'That's four times in as many minutes, and it's getting on my nerves. Besides, this is supposed to be a social occasion.'

'Sorry, Mr Lennox.'

'I guess that is an improvement,' he said drily as Charles Murray came panting in, full of apologies. Surely he hadn't expected her to call him Iain?

Dr Drimmon gave Charles no time to say more, or even get himself a drink before marshalling his team and calling out, 'Right! Let battle commence.'

Charles won the toss and put Essie in first. 'A brilliant psychological move,' he whispered to Lucy. 'You'll see.'

Without any hurry, Essie stepped up to the marker, removed her glasses, picked up a wood and, without seeming to take aim, decimated the target. Then back on with the glasses and back to her double Scotch and her *Nursing Mirror* left ready on the bar. This might be a social occasion, but Essie for one didn't mean to get carried away.

'What did I tell you?' crowed Charles. 'Our Essie may not be a bundle of laughs, but she's a terror with the woods. See David Drimmon's face?'

Charles was even happier with his tactics when David, still in shock, missed the target altogether. Then, just like Essie, Iain followed with a maximum score, which didn't surprise Lucy one bit. She'd already decided that Iain Lennox either did a thing superbly, or not at all. Being out of practice, she didn't shine herself to begin with, but, once she'd got her eye in, the orthopaedic team coasted home to a comfortable win.

The match over, all but Charles, who went back to the hospital, went over to the main building for a final refreshment, David Drimmon went straight to the phone and it was Iain Lennox who bought drinks all round. Essie, incongruous in her bright suit, but as sober as a judge, accepted her fourth Scotch of the evening before diving once more into her *Nursing Mirror*.

Iain put down another of Lucy's lime and ginger favourites on the table in front of her and slipped deftly into the seat beside her before David could. 'I must protect my staff,' he explained.

'And we need it, do we?'

'Are you saying you don't want to be protected? In that case, just say the word and I'll move.'

'No, thank you—he's not really my type.'

'And who is?'

Lucy leaned back against the padded velvet seat and said with studied dreaminess, 'A tall, blond Viking, with a beautiful Adam mansion, a six-figure income and one obsession. Me!'

'You don't want much, do you?'

Lucy couldn't help sending him a glance that sparked an answering gleam in the tawny eyes. 'So why do you think I'm still single?'

Iain Lennox dissolved into laughter, and, jammed together as they were on the cramped seat, the convulsive movements of his body were easily transmitted to Lucy. Which wasn't in the least unpleasant. Quite the reverse. A minute later he said, 'I hate to depress you, but you're not going to find your dream man in Glasgow.'

'Now he tells me!' wailed Lucy in accents of mock despair. 'Will it be all right if I hand in my notice at the end of the month, sir?'

'But can you afford to wait that long?' he wondered, still chuckling. 'After all, according to your application form, you'll never see twenty-four again.'

It was on the tip of Lucy's tongue to say, So what? Brunettes didn't fade as quickly as blondes, until she remembered that his current girlfriend was a blonde. Instead she said, 'Of course I lied about my age in order to get a senior post.'

'As long as that's all you lied about,' he returned just as the publican called time.

No, she'd told no lies, but she had concealed a fact

which, if revealed, would have been quite enough cause
for Iain Lennox to veto her appointment.

The party dispersed with chorused goodnights and
Lucy found herself walking across the car park with the
boss. 'You're very quiet,' he observed.

She started guiltily. 'I was thinking how difficult it
sometimes is to know what people are really like.' She
was thinking of him, but continued, 'For instance, I'd
never have thought that Essie Munro would be such a
devastating skittles player.' What an absolutely brilliant
piece of subterfuge, Luce! she told herself.

'Yes, isn't she fantastic? It's my belief that she's a
direct descendant of Sir Francis Drake.'

Lucy laughed obediently at such wit, but then, before
she could stop herself, she had said, 'You seem to be an
authority on ancestors.'

'I'm interested in genealogy, yes,' he returned surprisingly. 'But how did you know that?'

She'd averted disaster, only to plunge in deeper than
ever! 'Would you believe an inspired guess?' she tried
lightly.

'No,' said Iain Lennox.

Desperately Lucy searched for an explanation that
would put him off the scent. And then he said with overt
smugness, 'You've been asking questions about me.'

Was there ever such conceit? Clearly, nothing but the
truth would do now—but go canny, Lucy. 'Well then, I
haven't, Mr Lennox; I'd never be so—unsubtle. All the
same, I wish you hadn't persisted, because now I've got
to confess to eavesdropping.'

'Have you now? That's a pretty dire confession.'

'I realise that.' He hadn't sounded shocked, though.
Lucy ploughed on, 'It was when you were talking to Dr
Baird and I didn't dare to interrupt. Before my first ward
round. It was a Friday.'

'Yes, I do remember when the ward rounds are held, thank you. I remember that occasion well, but I can't remember discussing ancestry.'

'No, you weren't—well, not exactly. What you said was that—that somebody you both seemed to know must be descended from Attila the Hun. I d-didn't catch the person's name,' she added with what must surely be a stroke of pure genius. They had reached her car now and, thankfully, Lucy unlocked it.

'But of course!' he exclaimed. 'And there's only one person I know who fits that particular slot. We must have been talking about that new neighbour of yours whom you subsequently defended so stoutly—Ms Maggie Fearnan.'

'W-w-what a coincidence,' quavered Lucy.

'Yes, I suppose it was. Have you met her yet?'

Heavens, *what* a question! 'B-briefly,' she admitted.

'And now you agree with me about her,' he said with utter conviction.

'W-why do you say that, Mr L-Lennox?'

'One meeting, and already she's given you a stammer!' He went on chuckling with a self-satisfaction that was maddening as, after a casual goodnight, he strode away to his own car.

# CHAPTER THREE

'WOULD you say it was bending more today?' asked Mr Watson, gazing anxiously at his damaged knee.

'It certainly feels a little more willing to me,' Lucy answered cautiously. 'The range of movement is the same, but yes, I think it's a little more flexible.'

'Ah'm willing and a'—any time you like, Lucy,' called Kevin across the ward.

That'll teach me to choose my words more carefully, thought Lucy, knowing exactly what he meant. And how come they know my first name and this only my second week? 'In that case, *Mr McVeagh*, you may do all your exercises again, starting now,' she called back, to the obvious delight of Kevin's cronies.

'Told ye she'd have an answer, did I no'?'

'She's got ye there, Kev!'

Mr Walker asked over the backchat, 'Will ye be managing back, Miss Trent?'

'If I possibly can, but no promises, I'm afraid.' It was lunchtime and things had gone more smoothly this morning, with all the chesty patients improved and requiring fewer visits. Having arranged to have lunch with Essie Munro, Lucy went to see if she was ready.

'Miss Trent?' Lois Baird appeared in the doorway of the doctors' room. 'I'd like a word with you, please.'

'Certainly, Doctor.' Lucy followed her into the room, expecting to be told something about a patient.

'I hear that you stepped into my shoes last night,' Lois said accusingly.

'That's right—and I hope I played as well as you would have. Anyway, we won.'

'I heard that too; Charles was quite lyrical about your skill. But you do understand you were only standing in for me, I hope? I shall be playing next time.'

'Oh, yes, Mr Murray made that quite clear.'

'That's all right, then.' Lois cleared her throat. 'It's not only your skill at skittles I've been hearing about, so I think it's only fair to you to warn that you're wasting your time making eyes at Mr Lennox. He's already spoken for.'

And by you, of course—so that's what this is really all about! 'Dear me, is that how it looked? And I'd thought I was just being sociable,' Lucy retorted calmly. 'Now is there anything important about work you have to tell me, Doctor? Otherwise——'

'Don't you get smart with me, Miss Trent!'

'Getting smart, as you put it, is not my way,' Lucy answered quietly. 'Now will you excuse me, please?' And with that, she turned on her heel and marched out of the room. A senior physio didn't have to take that sort of thing from a houseman. All the same, it might have been wiser to handle Lois with more delicacy; less like Maggie Fearnan's daughter, in fact. You could have made yourself an enemy there, Lucy realised. Still, what harm can she possibly do to me?

'Message for you from Staff, Miss Trent,' said the student nurse she met in the corridor a moment later. 'She had an errand to run for Sister, so she's going straight to the canteen and will meet you there.'

Lucy thanked her automatically, still preoccupied with her run-in with Lois Baird.

'Well, did Lady Lois give you a bad time?' asked Essie curiously as she lifted her cardigan off the chair she'd been keeping for Lucy.

'Are you psychic as well as a skittles ace?' Lucy wondered.

'No.' Essie was a very literal person. 'But I heard she was gunning for you, so when I saw you looking so mad, I guessed.'

'I'm as mad with myself as I am with her,' confessed Lucy, having looked round to make sure nobody was likely to overhear. 'She seems to think I've got my eye on Mr Lennox, and I told her less tactfully than I might have done that I haven't, that's all.'

'All for you, perhaps, but not for her. She's been trotting after him ever since she came to the unit.' On Lucy's first day, Essie had told it the other way about!

'And is she getting anywhere?' asked Lucy—just for something to say, of course. She wasn't really interested.

'I've no idea, but I'd not be at all surprised. After all, if a normal red-blooded man gets it handed to him on a plate by a reasonably attractive female, he's not going to say no, is he?' Essie leaned forward, warming to her theme. 'It appears to me that most women find it fairly easy to get the man they fancy into bed. It's keeping him there exclusively when some other female muscles in that seems to be the difficulty. I know what you're thinking,' she went on, noting Lucy's astonishment, 'but onlookers see most of the game, don't forget.'

If Essie knew Lucy's thoughts, it was more than Lucy did. She was just amazed at hearing the earnest Essie advancing such a theory. 'I wouldn't say you've got it altogether wrong,' she returned slowly, 'but you make it sound as if men didn't have minds of their own.'

'Oh, they've got minds, all right, but it's their reflex bits that cause all the trouble.' Essie half stood up to peer at a passing tray. 'The cheesecake looks awful good today—I think I'll go and get some. Can I bring you anything else, Lucy?'

'No, thanks, I'll be having my main meal tonight with my mo—with my flatmate,' she substituted hastily. That was some theory of Essie's. And applied to the two people under discussion, probably not far out. No, that was unfair; just because she didn't like Lois, it didn't follow that men didn't find her very attractive. Lucy remembered the way Iain Lennox was inclined to smile at and tease the girl. And she sighed.

'May we?' Lucy looked up to see Charles Murray and Jim Carswell, the junior registrar.

'Please do. There's only Essie and myself at this table.'

'Good,' said Charles, and they both sat down. Charles proceeded to re-live last night's skittles triumph, being joined in that by Essie when she returned. Then Essie decided it was time to return to the unit as Sister would be on duty soon and would want a full report.

'Me too,' said Lucy, also scrambling to her feet.

'Aw, come on—you could spare us another five minutes of your charming company,' reckoned Charles with exaggerated pathos.

'In a year or two, perhaps—when I've dug myself in, but just now I've got a reputation for perfection to work on,' Lucy returned jokingly.

'That's a nice lassie—for a Sassenach,' she heard Jim Carswell say as she scampered after Essie.

Last week, it had been all Lucy could do to tell one grey-haired old lady from another, but now they were taking on distinct personalities. Take Mrs Fraser, for instance. She slept such a lot. No wonder she had developed a chest infection! 'Does Mrs Fraser sleep at night too, Trisha?' Lucy asked Kevin's girlfriend, whose bed was next.

'She does—and she snores.'

'Then this must be a hangover from her sleeping pills.'

'What pills?' wondered Trisha. 'It's us who has to take 'em—on account of her snoring. The dormouse is what me and Senga call her. Here, give me ma weight, and I'll do ma good leg lifts while you try 'er with the kiss o' life.'

If Mrs Fraser was a dormouse, then Mrs Moffat was like a wee robin; lively, intelligent and very curious. 'What brought you to Glasgow, Miss Trent?' she wanted to know today.

'I'm not quite sure, Mrs Moffat. I think it must be the gypsy in me.'

'I'm asking because you put me in mind of somebody, dear. It's something about the eyes, I think—and the determined way you set your jaw when you want us to try a bit harder at the exercises. Now whoever is it, I wonder?'

Immediately Lucy put on what Jock called her innocent baby look. Because this was Mrs Moffat's second fractured hip in six months, and last time she had been a patient of Ma's in the Northern General!

Then there was Mrs Dougal whose husband was getting very forgetful and was a great worry; Mrs Ross who had only come to Glasgow for a day's shopping and, as she said herself, had got more than she'd bargained for. Mrs Hamilton was a Jehovah's Witness who had sworn never to forgive her daughter for giving consent to that operation and the wicked blood transfusion that went with it, while her mother was still shocked and confused from the accident.

'So why do so many old ladies get these hip fractures?' asked Mrs Gifford, who had done her back in lifting her elderly father single-handed every time he fell.

Lucy thought. 'Well now, old people are often unsteady on their feet, so they fall more, and their bones are more brittle too. In women, this is partly due to hormonal changes in later life—and very often they don't get the right diet. Especially if they live alone, or are poor, or if cooking just gets to be too much trouble.'

She had been doing her best, but she hadn't held her patient's attention. Turning around to find out why, she saw Iain Lennox standing behind her. She coloured. 'Oh, gosh, sir, I'm sorry.' Because he might not approve of underlings handing out the kind of information that doctors usually did.

Her apology surprised him. 'You don't have to be, Miss Trent. I couldn't have put it better myself. And if Mrs Gifford should fall and fracture her upper extremity of femur in forty or fifty years' time, we'll know it's not your fault.'

Mrs Gifford giggled delightedly at this flattering underestimation of her age as Mr Lennox drew Lucy aside and asked, 'So how's it going, Lucy?'

Lucy! 'Fine, sir, thank you. Though I am rather concerned about Mrs Fraser. She wasn't very lively yesterday, but today I had trouble keeping her awake long enough to do her exercises. Is she on tranquillisers or something else that might——?'

She stopped because he was frowning hard. 'None that I have prescribed, but thank you for bringing this to my notice. I shall look into it.' He looked round as Lois came pattering into the ward.

She glared at Lucy before cooing breathlessly, 'Oh, Iain, I'm so sorry. Nobody told me you were on the unit.'

'Probably because nobody saw me sneaking up the back stairs,' he returned reasonably. 'Still, now you are here, perhaps you wouldn't mind chaperoning me while I examine the new admission. I was just about to ask Miss Trent, but I'm sure she'd rather get on with her treatments.'

'Chaperoning's more my job than hers,' Lucy heard Lois say petulantly as she returned to Mrs Gifford's bedside.

'You did those extension exercises so well yesterday that I think we might include some harder ones today. . .'

Next on the list was Trisha—some more knee-bending exercises were what she needed most. Another round of the chests—and yes, there might just be time to give Mr Watson that extra session he'd asked for. . .

As Lucy was passing the open door of the office on her way back to the men's side, Sister Clyde called her in. 'I just wondered if you'd care to tell me over a cup of tea how you're settling down, Miss Trent?'

At the risk of finishing late again, this was not an invitation to be turned down. 'Thank you very much, Sister. That would be lovely,' smiled Lucy.

The tea poured, Sister put Lucy at her ease by telling her all about her first grandchild, before leading gradually into a professional discussion. There were no divergencies of opinion, and Lucy learned a lot about the unit by the time Sister moved on to personal matters. 'I hope we're not keeping you too busy to see something of your relatives, my dear,' she said.

'Oh, no, Sister. There's always the weekends.'

'Your mother's family, I expect.' Lucy realised her unease must be showing when Sister expanded gently, 'As you have an English name and have been living in England, I naturally assumed that it's your mother who has the Scottish connections.'

'Yes, Sister, that's right,' Lucy was saying when all the doctors poured into the office.

'You heard the rattle of teacups,' challenged Sister with a smile.

'Actually, I wanted to discuss Mrs Fraser, but now

that you mention it. . .' Iain Lennox gave Sister one of his rare smiles.

Sister topped up the pot. 'You were saying, Mr Lennox?'

'We think that Mrs Fraser is hyper-thyroid, Sister.' He turned to Lucy. 'Thanks for alerting us, Miss Trent—well done!'

He might think so, but Sister was frowning, so in case she thought that Lucy was out of line Lucy said hastily, 'It was really the patients on either side of her who drew my attention.' Had that made it better or worse? 'Thanks very much for the tea, Sister—now I'd better get back to work. That knee of Mr Watson's. . .' She got herself out of the room, feeling unaccountably nervous. She had intended keeping a very low profile until she'd assessed all staff attitudes, and she hadn't managed it. That's Maggie coming out in me, she decided ruefully.

'Most assuredly,' she had heard Mr Lennox say as she closed the office door. In answer to some murmured comment of Sister's, she suspected, and she'd have given a lot to know what she had said.

Lucy was still worrying about it all when, her work done, she began her homeward journey. So when she noticed Mr Lennox waving to her so vigorously from a bus queue, she pulled in to the kerb half expecting a rocket. Are you going daft? she wondered the next minute. He's not going to discipline you in the street; besides, he praised you, didn't he?

He thrust his bright head in through the open window and asked hopefully, 'Are you by any chance going straight home? Because if so, I'd be very grateful for a lift.'

When Lucy said, 'Certainly, sir,' he opened the nearside door and got into the passenger seat. 'My car's been in for a service and I'm just going to pick it up,' he explained as he fastened the seatbelt. 'The garage is just around the corner from your flats. You don't mind?' he asked belatedly.

Lucy only just managed to smile as she responded, 'Of course not, sir. Only too glad to be of service.' Because she had this feeling that she was soon to be found out. She hadn't bargained for being seen driving Maggie's sternest opponent round Maggie's part of town!

'Nice car,' Iain was saying. 'And brand new too, I see. Have you won the pools, or what?'

'My mother gave it to me.' Damn! She needn't have told him that. Yet why should admitting to having a mother be suspect? Nearly everybody her age had one.

'So you have a very kind and generous mother.'

'Indeed I have.' Despite her anxiety, Lucy was delighted to be able to pay Maggie that tribute.

'So why did you take this job, then? I thought good mother-and-daughter relationships were out of fashion.'

'I don't see the connection,' returned Lucy cautiously. That had sounded as if he knew something!

'It obviously wasn't to get away from home that you came running up to Scotland. Was it man trouble, then?'

It's all right, Luce—he thinks your mother's down south. She began to breathe more freely. With what she hoped was a careless shrug, she said, 'When does any women not have man trouble? But as I told you at my interview, I just wanted a change, and Scotland seemed like a good idea on account of my Scottish connections.' And now we'll have a change of subject Mr Lennox, sir, if you don't mind. 'You don't drive a British car, then, Mr Lennox.'

'You *are* observant,' he said teasingly.

'Not really, but the garage near the flats only sells Audis and VWs.'

'Just as I said, you're very observant. Especially as you've only just moved in.'

Could he possibly suspect her of a longer, unacknowledged connection with the area? Stop it, Lucy, you're getting paranoid! she told herself. 'I rather pride myself on my powers of observation,' she said. Oh, dear, that had sounded conceited.

'You used them to good effect for Mrs Fraser,' he remarked.

'I do hope Sister didn't mind about that,' Lucy returned quickly, remembering her earlier doubts.

'Mind? Why ever would she? Actually, she was rather impressed.'

'That's a relief. She's such a nice person—I wouldn't want to annoy or upset her.'

'The only thing that upsets Sister Clyde is shoddy work, so on present showing you're quite safe from her wrath. Forgive me for pointing it out, but it would have been much quicker if you'd turned left back there.'

Thereby driving right past the Northern at a time when Maggie could be driving out and spotting them together? Not likely!

'You have a most expressive face, Miss Lucy Trent, which just at the moment is suggesting to me that your thoughts are not pleasant,' Iain Lennox remarked.

'I—I forgot to buy anything for supper,' she improvised wildly.

'Is that all? I was half afraid you were planning a murder! There's a Safeway half a block beyond my garage. But I expect, being observant, you've already noticed that.'

'N-no, I hadn't. Thank you very much for telling me.'

'Not at all.' He paused. 'Isn't it a good thing you're giving me this lift? Otherwise you might have gone hungry.'

'Absolutely,' breathed Lucy, rather pleased to discover that he was flirting with her in a mild sort of way, yet relieved to see the garage just ahead.

When she drew in to the kerb, he said, 'I'm most grateful.'

'No, really—I was very glad to help.'

'How very polite we are,' he said with an engaging grin which Lucy knew she ought to resist, but couldn't. She smiled back, but tried not to let it get out of hand.

'Perhaps I can be of service to you some time,' he hoped then. Would he never get out of the car? Suppose Ma should come along? This was where she bought her petrol!

But at last he unfastened his seatbelt and said, 'I really mustn't keep you from buying your supper any longer.' Once on the pavement, he bent down to say, 'Thanks again, Lucy. See you tomorrow.'

'Yes—goodbye for now, then, sir.' The minute he shut the passenger door, she accelerated away like a rally driver.

Lucy had promised Maggie mince and tatties for supper, but once in the supermarket, she found herself buying things like fillet steak, broccoli and early strawberries—all things that Ma adored. And all because she was feeling disloyal for giving a lift to one of her mother's most bitter critics. And why had she picked up this bottle of wine as well when she knew Ma was on call and wouldn't drink anything? Less than a fortnight of deceit and subterfuge, and already she was a nervous wreck!

Having overspent so recklessly, Lucy had to write a cheque for her purchases.

When Maggie crashed into the flat in her usual uninhibited style, the meal was almost ready. She stood in the kitchen doorway and sniffed appreciatively. 'Netta's mince never smells like this. Whatever have you done to it, Luce?'

'I've changed the menu. I was a bit late and—and this was quicker.' Did that count as Lying to your Mother, or Sparing her Feelings? 'Actually, I decided to give you a treat.' If you were going to tell lies, then they might as well be big ones.

'Lucy, you old sentimentalist!' Maggie peered under the grill, then spun round purring. 'I'm just beginning to realise the benefit of having one's daughter for a flatmate,' she enthused. 'Let's hope the local inhabitants refrain from injuring themselves long enough for me to eat this wonderful banquet!'

Obligingly they did, and after dinner, Lucy carried the coffee tray out on to the balcony, which faced north-west, towards the setting sun and Ben Lomond. Her mother was lounging in a deckchair wearing sunglasses and a disgraceful old straw hat of her father's. 'Coffee and mints, Ma?'

Maggie sat up and gazed reverently at the box. 'Bendicks! If I didn't know you better, my child, I'd think you'd got a guilty secret.'

Lucy slopped coffee into a saucer with a hand that shook. At that very moment, she'd been trying to decide whether or not there had been an unspoken message in Iain Lennox's eyes when he'd said goodbye. And if that wasn't a guilty secret. . .!

Ma was looking at her expectantly. She had to say something. 'I'm afraid people are beginning to suspect, Ma,' she said.

Maggie got the point right away. 'Don't be silly, Luce. You're only imagining that, because you're not ready for the truth to be known.'

'I've been asked an awful lot of questions.'

'Like what—and by whom?' asked Maggie sharply.

'Sister Clyde and Iain Lennox, mostly. Why did I do physio? Is it because my mother is one? How do I get on with her? That sort of thing.'

'Is that all they ever say?'

'No—there's plenty of other stuff as well, but——'

'Sounds to me like ordinary, natural curiosity about a newcomer. What's commonly known as taking an interest. And the only reason it makes you uncomfortable is that you know something you don't want them to find out.'

'You could be right, Ma.'

'I'm sure I am. Now pour me another coffee before it goes cold, there's a love. I shall have to go back to the hospital fairly soon.'

Maggie had been gone some time, checking on a patient she was particularly concerned about, before Lucy remembered Mrs Moffat. She had discerned a physical resemblance between Lucy and Ms Maggie Fearnan, her one-time surgeon. Lucy was sure of it. And if she had, then Iain Lennox, who knew her mother so much better than Mrs Moffat did, might very well do the same before long. He might already be suspecting. That, and not a dawning attraction, could be the reason why she had caught him looking at her so often during that drive.

# CHAPTER FOUR

THURSDAY evening, and Lucy was standing quietly by while the anaesthetist in charge of intensive care checked the patient. 'You've done a good job,' he said at last. 'The right lung is quite clear now, so I think we should leave him to rest until morning.'

'Thank you, Doctor.' So, barring emergencies, Lucy's first evening session at the Glasgow General Hospital was over. She was grateful. It had been a very busy day as usual. So had the evening. It was now almost ten, and the prospect of remaining on duty all night as well had been unattractive, to say the least. At St Crispin's, they managed things better. But at St Crispin's they also had more staff.

As she returned to Physiotherapy to change out of uniform, Lucy was wondering if Iain Lennox had also finished work. They had met on the hospital's main staircase about half an hour earlier. 'Fancy seeing you!' they had exclaimed simultaneously, and then they had both laughed.

After which, Iain said, 'Perhaps we should work nights more often. I haven't seen you to talk to for ages.'

Two days, to be precise. Not since she had set him down outside his garage on Tuesday. Any instructions and information had come to her from Charles, and Lucy had been mildly surprised to discover that she minded that.

In the car park soon afterwards, they ran into each other for the second time that evening. When Iain fell into step beside her, Lucy said lightly, 'Don't tell me—you're needing another lift.'

'What I am needing,' he returned, 'is an hour or so of gentle unwinding—and somebody sympathetic to share it with.'

'I'm very sympathetic,' claimed Lucy almost without thought. 'Everybody says so.'

'I suspected as much, and I know the very place.'

It was three minutes' walk at the most to a quietly luxurious and old-fashioned hotel with a cocktail lounge that was uncrowded and discreet. Iain commandeered a secluded corner, after ordering coffee, sandwiches and fruit. 'I missed dinner,' he explained as they sat down.

'Me too,' volunteered Lucy.

'What a lot we have in common,' he said in the same half humorous, half teasing tone that had characterised everything he had said so far tonight.

'Like a neglected diet, work—and more work?'

'Yes, work does sometimes get in the way, does it not? Not that I'd ever want to do anything else,' he added quickly.

'Nor would I.'

'Because you like to be useful,' he teased, and they laughed together again, remembering.

Lucy slipped off her jacket and laid it over the arm of her chair. 'Have you any idea how much you scared me that day?'

'Did I really? You gave no sign of it.'

'I should hope not!'

'You're proud,' he discovered. 'All right, so why did you take the job if you thought I was such an ogre?'

'I hoped I could live with it, having heard that Mr Dunning was—rather less terrifying.'

He glowered at her with pretended ferocity. 'Clearly

somebody has been blackening my character in a scandalous manner.'

Not scandalous; merely honest, according to Lucy's informant. Aloud she said, 'Nobody needed to. You scared me quite adequately all by yourself.'

The look he gave her then would have unsettled any woman under forty. 'And are you still scared of me, Miss Lucy Trent?' he asked in a velvety voice.

'Less than I was,' revealed Lucy with commendable cool. 'In fact, I'm beginning to wonder if your bark might not be worse than your bite.'

'As well as being sympathetic, you're also very perceptive,' he said. 'Now eat your supper before they decide it's time to throw us out.'

As they walked back to the hospital, Iain tucked Lucy's arm through his, something she was prepared to admit to finding rather nice. 'How do you like to spend your spare time?' he asked casually.

Aha! So you *are* interested! 'Let me see now—I play skittles, of course.'

'I know that. And?'

'I like going to concerts—and the theatre. I also take long country walks. Nothing out of the ordinary.'

'And do you do these ordinary things alone, or in company?'

'I prefer to have company. A girl out by herself is liable to be misunderstood.'

He laughed and pressed her arm closer to his side for a second before releasing her as they reached her car. 'I like the way you put things,' he said. 'Now tell me, do your varied tastes extend to sailing?'

Pretending not to notice where all this was leading, Lucy had taken out her car keys and unlocked the door. 'I used to crew for my grandfather until his arthritis forced him to give up sailing.' Not too risky an admission, surely? There must be many arthritic grandfathers in Scotland.

'But do you like sailing or not? You didn't include it in your list.'

'Only because I haven't had the chance to sail much these last few years. I love it, though.'

Hands clasped together and one elbow resting on the roof of Lucy's car, Iain looked quizzically down at her and asked, 'Enough to go sailing with me on Saturday?'

Careful now, Lucy Trent. . . 'Much as I should enjoy that, it's only fair to warn you that I must be rather rusty.'

'It'll all come back to you, once you get a rope in your hands again,' Iain asserted confidently.

'I'd like to think so, but supposing it doesn't? I'd hate to spoil your day.'

'If I'd thought you might do that, I'd not have asked you. Anyway, you'll find I'm very good at giving orders.'

'I've kind of noticed that already,' she told him with a tiny smile.

'I'll overlook that,' he said, 'but only because I really do need a good crewman—if you'll forgive the chauvinism.'

'I'm very forgiving—thanks to all the practice I've had.'

'Yet another good quality to add to a growing list,' he observed thoughtfully. 'But nobody's perfect, so there has to be a flaw in you somewhere. I wonder what it is?'

Oh, man, if you only knew! 'Let's see now. I've got a bit of a temper. I don't lose it all that often, but when I do, the windows rattle.' In fact, I'm very like my mother in that respect! she thought.

'That's quite all right,' said Iain. 'I like a woman with spirit. Except for one or two notable exceptions.'

And there'd be no prizes for guessing the identity of one! 'Good, I shall stop worrying, then,' returned Lucy ironically. 'Where do you keep your boat?' she asked, hoping to steer the conversation into safer channels.

'At Balloch, on Loch Lomond. So if I were to pick you up around nine, we could be on the water within the hour.'

Less than five miles from the cottage, damn it! Why couldn't he sail out of one of the upper Clyde resorts? And as for picking her up—with Maggie's nameplate on the door? 'I'll meet you in the forecourt—to save you the trouble of getting out of the car,' insisted Lucy.

'Another instance of her thoughtfulness,' marvelled Iain. 'But I'm not quite as decrepit as the folk she spends her days treating.' As if to prove that, he slipped an arm around her waist and cupped her chin with his free hand.

His kiss was skilful, unhurried and very, very nice. It was also rather disturbing, and Lucy was glad rather than sorry that he didn't repeat it.

'I take your point,' she contrived rather breathlessly. 'All the same, I will meet you out front—it'll save time.'

'Eager,' he said provocatively. 'I like that. A pity, but I suppose I'd better let you go now. Drive carefully, and don't be late for work tomorrow. We have to present you for Mr Dunning's approval before the round.'

'Ah, yes—the round,' Lucy echoed as he released her. Was it really only a fortnight since the first one?

Essie put her head round the cubicle curtain just as Lucy was resettling Mrs Dorward after treatment. 'They're here—in Sister's office,' she said cryptically, before disappearing again.

Lucy smiled at her patient. 'What a good thing we're

finished, then. But I'll be back to see you again after the round.'

'Ye neednae bother,' retorted the old lady. She couldn't understand all this fuss about a chest which, she was tired of telling them, had been brim fu' these past thirty years.

When Lucy met Tom Dunning's keen glance across the office, there was no surprise there—just polite interest. So Ma had been successful in reaching him before he returned to work. When Iain introduced her, Tom's quiet, 'Welcome to the General, Miss Trent,' was just right. 'I hope you'll enjoy working here,' he added.

'Thank you very much, sir. I certainly have so far,' answered Lucy, being careful not to look at Iain, while pretty sure he was looking at her.

They began as usual in the men's ward, with Kevin. 'I've just been looking at your latest X-rays,' Tom said to him. 'That femur is looking very good.'

Kevin promptly launched into his usual spiel about having to spend so long in bed because they hadn't pinned it together.

'Pinning would have been both inappropriate and dangerous,' said Tom levelly. 'Such injuries as yours can easily become infected. There's one well-documented case which ended with the patient having his leg amputated through the hip joint, though not in Britain, I'm glad to say.'

He had dealt with Kevin quite as well as Iain had done, and Lucy began to believe her mother's insistence that Tom was the only man who could quell her with a look.

Both Mike Craig and George Wilson were patients of Tom's. 'I hope you're keeping those quads going and giving passive movement to the patella, Miss Trent.'

'Yes, I am, sir,' Lucy answered.

Mr Watson was next. He was Iain's patient. 'Any problems here?' he asked, smiling.

'None, sir, though we both wish the knee were bending better.'

'Then you're both expecting too much. Thirty degrees in one week is very good going, considering the severity of the injury.'

'Thank you, sir.'

There was also praise for Mr Govan's marked improvement. 'The swelling is subsiding well. What about the pain?' Iain asked him.

'Likewise, sir,' reported the patient. 'Miss Trent's a rare wee wonder.'

'I'm sure we all agree with that,' returned Iain, while Lois glowered as if to show that agreement was not unanimous.

Tom was already with the next patient. 'Dr Baird, this man's traction was slack. I've fixed it, but remember I like them all checked daily, please.'

Lois opened her mouth to protest, caught Charles's warning glance and returned a meek, 'Yes, sir.'

Mr Johnstone was discharged. Quite apart from his cheerful personality, Lucy would miss his assistance with surly Mr Aitken. Who would jolly him along for her now?

The next patient, Mr Duncan, was one of yesterday's ops cases. 'An Austen-Moore prosthesis,' Iain bent down to whisper. 'I did a posterior approach, so no flexion for a week, please, Lucy.'

'I'll remember—sir.'

Another glare for Lucy when Lois noted the looks accompanying that exchange. Remember what I told you, she seemed to be signalling.

Mr Buchan was next. 'There's a slight flexion deformity of the hip here, Miss Trent,' said Tom.

'I know, sir, but to counteract it, Mr Buchan is spending as much time as possible lying prone.'

'The physio puts a weight on ma bum as well, sir. And ma stump's a lovely shape now. D'ye wish to see it?' asked the patient.

'Please.'

'That contracture was there before Miss Trent came to us, Tom,' said Iain as they moved on.

'I know that, but we can't have the lassie thinking that we're not bothered about it, can we?'

Oh yes, Tom, thought Lucy, you're doing fine. Nobody would guess that you're one of my mother's oldest friends.

It was agreed that Tom would take over Calum Sinclair and his dislocated hip, if Iain kept Bill McInnes and his fractured pelvis. Except for the occasional twinge, both of them were over the discomfort of their fractured ribs. 'If only all bones would heal as quickly as ribs, we could cut the waiting list for elective surgery at a stroke,' Tom observed wryly as they left the ward. 'Still, that was some marathon session you and Charles had yesterday, Iain. A hip replacement, the Austen-Moore, two repairs to cruciate ligaments, three meniscectomies—and that's only in the men's ward.' He glanced towards the bed in the corner, remembering another patient. 'Tell me, have you written up young Tim Simmonds for the *Journal* yet?'

He was the young man whose crushed foot Iain had reconstructed so wonderfully.

'And how do you think I found the time to write articles with you off fishing?' wondered Iain.

'Can I take that to mean you intend going the whole summer without a holiday afloat?' Tom retaliated.

'Take no notice, Miss Trent,' instructed Sister. 'Our consultants are really the best of friends.'

'Yes, Sister.' Lucy was wondering less about that than how Tom reacted if or when Iain ran Maggie down in his hearing. And while on the subject of reactions, what would be Maggie's when she discovered that her daughter planned to spend a day sailing with one of her foes? But then hadn't Ma told her to be charming? She'd just been more successful than either of them had expected, that was all. And of course Lucy was going to tell her mother—at the right moment.

'Stand by for Phase Two!' called Charles as he helped Sister to push the trolley into the women's ward.

Mrs Barr first; she who, in the Geriatric Unit, had managed to climb over her protective bedrails. She looked to be trying the same thing here, only Sister had been too smart for her. As well as rails, Mrs Barr's bed was barricaded with chairs. When she saw them coming, she gave Iain a beautiful smile and said, 'Open this gate for me, son. Ma wee dug is needin' a walk.'

Quick as a flash he answered, 'You stay where you are, hen. It's raining, so I'll take him out for you.' Then in an aside to Sister, 'Would she not be safer up and sitting in one of the special chairs?'

'She is most of the time, but while giving her a bath this morning, one of my nurses noted some abdominal tenderness, so we put her back to bed so that you could examine her more easily.'

Tom promptly asked the doctors' standard question in such circumstances. 'Is she constipated, Sister?'

Sister said anything but, and as nobody else was similarly affected, she didn't think it was just a bug going the rounds. Both consultants then examined Mrs Barr, though not without much protesting. Clearly she suspected them of dire designs on her person. There was nothing seriously wrong as far as they could tell, but it

was agreed to get the opinion of a general surgeon if the
trouble didn't soon clear up.

'How are you managing with her, Miss Trent?' wondered Tom.

'Very well, sir. We have some strange conversations,
but as activity is the one thing Mrs Barr craves, I'm
having no difficulty getting her going.'

'But it's a different story here, I fancy,' observed
Tom, watching Mrs Fraser, eyes closed, gently swaying
in her chair.

Iain explained their suspicions and how they were
awaiting the results of tests carried out, and they moved
on to Mrs Ross, who was pronounced fit enough for
transfer to the cottage hospital near her home.

Mrs Dorward continued grumpy and Mrs Dougal was
still anxious about her husband, who was being cared for
in a home, pending her discharge. Poor Mrs Hamilton
remained convinced that the proverbial rich man stood a
better chance of heaven than she did. 'Faith can move
mountains, but unfortunately, it's not always as successful at fixing broken bones unaided,' observed Iain
soothingly.

'Lucky for you, then, or you'd be out of a job!' she
retorted smartly.

'There's no answer to that,' he sighed in Lucy's ear,
causing her to choke on a suppressed giggle.

Mrs Moffat couldn't wait for them to get to her bed
because she'd remembered who it was Lucy reminded
her of. 'It's that woman in charge at the North——'

'British Hotel? Yes, I've noticed it too, Mrs Moffat,'
Tom interposed swiftly. 'But now let's see if you're well
enough to go home, shall we?' Fortunately Mrs Moffat
was so enchanted at that prospect that she quite forgot
what she'd intended to say. Lucy breathed more easily.

'Nearly half our female beds taken up by unfortunate

old ladies with fractured hips,' said Tom in layman's language as they moved on. 'Still, if hormone replacement therapy really takes off, then this could be the last generation to suffer thus.'

Murmurs of hope all round—especially from the women!—as the team moved on to the first of yesterday's operation cases. 'Torn cartilages are for footballers,' said Tom, 'so how did you get yours, Miss Grant?'

'Playing football, sir.'

'Ask a silly question,' he murmured. 'You might have warned me, Iain.'

'Not likely! She caught me out in exactly the same way. How's she doing, Miss Trent?'

'I'm bound to say that her quads are contracting better than those of any of the men who were in theatre yesterday, Mr Lennox.'

'My dear Miss Trent, I do hope you're not a feminist,' he returned sadly.

'Perish the thought, sir!'

Smiles all round, except from Lois, who was beside herself with rage at such raillery.

Bilateral excision of bunions next—one patient who wouldn't be needing physio, thank goodness.

Then three youngsters in a row—Trisha and her fractured tibia, mending slowly, Senga with something similar and also doing well, and then Betty Teviot, a fourteen-year-old who had had a cartilagenous cyst removed from her knee.

Once the round was over, Lucy said she would have to forgo Sister's lovely coffee and make up for lost time. Lois was delighted, while Iain looked disappointed. Tom said fine, but could she please spare him a few minutes at lunchtime? He added that he would be in his consulting-room.

In the ward, Kevin was inclined to play up even more

than usual, but soon settled to work when Lucy said that
if he didn't, she wouldn't be bringing Trisha through in
a wheelchair for an afternoon visit. Then she dealt with
the class in record time to make sure she had time for
the ops cases.

'Yes, Mr Watson, Mr Lennox was pleased with your
knee, but there's still a long way to go yet. Oh, dear, is
that the lunch-trolley already?'

When Lucy knocked on the door of Tom's room and
looked round it, he was dictating answers to all the
letters which had accumulated during his absence. He
switched off the machine when he saw her and got up to
give her a congratulatory hug and a kiss. 'Well done,
Luce! What a good thing I was away so that Iain had to
interview you. Having chosen you, he can hardly start
finding fault when he discovers who you are.'

'That's right,' agreed Lucy, feeling ever so slightly
guilty. Only this time she felt she was being disloyal to
Iain. Was there ever such a problem?

Tom hadn't finished. 'Had he known you were
Maggie's daughter, he would have been prejudiced
against you, simply because they don't hit it off.' He
smiled roguishly. 'But from what I've seen this morning,
I'd say you've absolutely nothing to worry about. He
could hardly keep his eyes off you during the round—
much to Lois Baird's annoyance!'

'Well, after all, she is the present girlfriend, isn't she?'
Tom was sure to know.

'Present may well be the wrong tense now,' he
returned with a knowing grin. 'Iain's a nice laddie, but a
mite too attractive for his own good. The lassies won't
leave him alone and it's made him a trifle over-confident
in that department.'

That fits in with Essie's unflattering estimate and the
speed with which he's moved in on me, Lucy decided.

'Well, it would, wouldn't it?' she agreed casually before changing the subject. 'Tom, you were wonderful this morning—coming to the rescue like that when Mrs Moffat fingered me!'

'It seemed the best thing to do in the circumstances.' He paused. 'But she's not the only one to spot the likeness, Lucy. Sister Clyde saw it almost at once, and she tackled me about it first thing this morning.'

'I knew all those questions meant something, but how. . .?' Lucy began.

'She and Maggie worked together years ago, just after the divorce. She said it was just like watching the young Maggie all over again when you squared up to Iain so nobly on your first day when he wasn't being too complimentary about your mother.'

'I hadn't realised we were so much alike,' Lucy sighed. 'And if Sister and Mrs Moffat can see it, then it can only be a matter of time before Iain—before Mr Lennox does too.'

'Not necessarily. He never knew the young and beautiful Maggie.'

Neither did Mrs Moffat! 'Sister won't tell, will she?' asked Lucy anxiously.

'No. She knows all about the antipathy between Maggie and Iain, and when I said you wanted to get and keep your job on your own merits, she understood at once.' Tom glanced at his watch and Lucy said tactfully that she ought to be going.

By now all the patients would have had their lunch, so she decided not to waste time having some herself.

In the men's ward, a noisy game of Brag was in progress, with Kevin's bed in use as a table. 'Sorry about this, chaps,' said Lucy, 'but first things first. I want Mr Watson—and you too, Mr Buchan—and as for you, Mr

Lanark, you shouldn't be out of bed at all, when you only had your cartilage removed yesterday.'

'Give us half an hour, hen,' said Kevin, continuing to deal.

'I can't, I don't have the time to waste.'

'Ach, awa' an' put yer feet up!'

Lucy saw red. 'How dare you?' she roared, astonishing herself. 'Don't you realise I have to work hours extra every day, just to get through the work? You three, get back to your beds at once!' She had never snapped at them before, which was probably why it worked like a charm.

'Ma knee's awful painful,' moaned Bob Lanark when Lucy told him he wasn't trying hard enough to tighten his muscles.

'Well, if you will disobey orders, what else can you expect?' she asked crisply.

'Ye're a hard wumman and no mistake.'

'Being soft wouldn't get me far with you lot. Now then, five minutes' practice every hour, mind—and as I'm psychic, I shall know if you don't do it. Now then, Mr Duncan, I'm going to fold back your bedclothes, so that I can watch you doing your foot exercises while I redo Mr Buchan's bandage.'

'You're like a juggler, Miss T,' was the comment.

It was almost three before Lucy got to the women's ward. Would she manage to get them all treated by six o'clock supper? Mrs Moffat would be one less, but there were still three new ones from yesterday's ops list. Thank goodness there weren't any really bad chests now. . .

'Lucy? I'm Sally Lawson and I'll be helping you in the afternoons from Monday on, so Mrs Cumnock has sent me over to get orientated.'

Lucy spun round with a wide smile to assure the girl she was as welcome as the flowers in May.

'Aw, shucks, you're only saying that. Now what would you like me to do?' Just like Lucy, Sally was no time-waster. They would get on just fine.

'Leaving already? You're slacking, Miss Trent.' Iain Lennox's teasing words floated out through the open door of Sister's office as Lucy was passing.

She checked and went in. 'Is it really only five-thirty? My watch must be fast.' She smiled at him impishly. 'Actually I've been given some help—at last.'

'I know—I saw her. She looks a nice lassie.'

'She is very nice. And competent too. She's also married,' added Lucy.

'Now why did you tack on that last bit?' he wondered, smiling at her exactly as he had smiled at Lois Baird that first morning. So she really was flavour of the month, then.

'Just telling the boss all I've found out so far about the newest addition to the team,' she returned, meeting the challenge in the tawny eyes with a challenging look of her own.

'So when do I get to meet this paragon?'

'Sally went back to the department some time ago, so it'll be Monday now, I'm afraid. If only I'd known you were dying to meet her. . .'

'It's all right—I can wait, now I know she's married,' he answered provocatively. 'Are you staying for tea? Sister's away to fill the kettle.'

'Any chance of a biscuit with it?' wondered Lucy pathetically. 'I had to miss lunch again.'

Iain frowned. 'This has to stop, Lucy. You must take a break, no matter how busy you are.'

'I will, now that I'm getting help.'

'Just mind that you do.'

'Yes, sir,' Lucy was answering meekly, when Sister came back.

Judging by her expression, she had assumed that Lucy was being reprimanded. She bent reproving eyes on Iain before saying, 'Working overtime yet again, Miss Trent? Would you like a cup of tea before you go?'

'Yes, please, Sister.' When Sister went to her special cupboard for another cup, Iain winked at Lucy behind her back.

But when Sister produced some rich-looking fruit cake as well, he said, 'You're very honoured, Lucy. She never brings that out for me.'

'Miss Trent went without lunch again today, Mr Lennox. I notice these things.'

'But then you don't miss much at all, do you, Jenny Clyde?'

'I'm not paid to miss things,' she retorted. But so far she seemed to have missed his change of female interest!

Iain barely had time to drink his tea before Essie appeared in the doorway to say that Betty Teviot's mother was wondering if she could have a word with him. 'Of course, Staff. She was convinced that Betty's cyst was malignant,' he explained to them all, 'so I shall have great pleasure in telling her it was nothing of the sort. After that, I have to see a patient in Surgical Four, Sister, should you need me.' Then he looked at Lucy. 'Have a nice weekend, Miss Trent. Are you doing anything exciting?'

'I'm going sailing tomorrow, sir, but whether that will be exciting remains to be seen.'

Determined to have the last word he said, 'I'm sure it will be—if you've chosen the right companion.' Then he hurried off after Essie.

Lucy was deciding that whatever happened, tomorrow

certainly would not be dull, when Sister asked, 'More cake, Miss Trent—Lucy?'

'Yes, please, Sister—it's very good. Did you make it?'

'Grateful patient,' explained Sister, going on to ask, 'Any problems, apart from the obvious one of too much to do and not enough time?'

'Everything's fine, thank you—especially as from Monday, I'm to have help in the afternoons.' Lucy hesitated. 'Tom Dunning tells me that you know who I am, Sister.'

'I guessed he would—I hope he also told you that your secret is safe with me.'

'Yes, he did. And I'm glad that you know. It's not that I'm ashamed or—or anything. . .'

'Of course not! You just don't want anybody thinking you only got this job because of your family connections.'

What tact, marvelled Lucy, as she thanked Sister for her understanding. 'And thanks for the tea too. I think I might just make it home now.'

'Have a nice weekend, dear—and please remember me to your mother. You may also tell her that I think you're just as hard a worker as she is.'

'Praise indeed,' said Lucy, much pleased. 'Thank you again—and I'll certainly pass on your message.'

# CHAPTER FIVE

JUST in case Iain should come up to the flat with her that evening, the last thing Lucy did before leaving was to stick a card with her name on it over Maggie's nameplate on the door. And last night she had removed telltale articles like text books and photographs from the living-room to Maggie's bedroom. Provided she could keep Iain from examining the entryphone list, and they didn't meet some gossipy body on the stairs, she should be safe. Of course, he might not want to come up. A full day of each other's company might prove to be quite enough for both of them!

It was a much nicer day than the weather forecast had suggested. The sky was cloudless and already the air was quite warm on Lucy's bare arms. She looked up at the trees. They were still. So the only question was whether there would be enough breeze to fill the sails.

Iain was prompt to the second. Perfect timing—or had he been waiting around the corner, out of sight, so as not to seem too eager? Don't be silly, Lucy. That's a girl's trick.

He didn't get out of the car, but opened the door for her from the inside. 'Hi there, Lucy.' He took her jacket and big canvas holdall and tossed them into the back. A swift appraisal of her deck shoes, shorts, striped shirt and bright scarf holding back her abundant and shining dark hair. 'A photo-call vision in red, white and blue,' he said with approval. 'I do hope you don't fall in!'

'I second that,' returned Lucy as she got into the car.

Her turn to comment now. 'And you're looking rather——'

'Disgraceful? I know.'

'Workmanlike, is what I was going to say.' Another glance at his dark shorts and striped cotton T-shirt. 'But now that you've said it. . .'

'You sure know how to boost a guy's ego,' he returned in a passable transatlantic accent.

'I hope so—when it's necessary.'

'Which you obviously do not consider is now.'

'Your ego seems in pretty good shape to me—as well it might be.'

A quizzical glance which Lucy withstood, wide-eyed and guileless. 'I'll take that at face value,' Iain decided as they set off.

'Good,' approved Lucy. 'Because I was only speaking the truth.' Yes, you are the least bit conceited, she thought, but with rather more justification than most. How many ways there were of saying more or less the same thing! 'I'm really looking forward to the day,' she said next; a simple, straightforward truth this time.

'Then that makes two of us,' concluded Iain.

'What sort of a boat do you have?' she asked.

'An Enterprise class at Balloch, but I've a part share in an eight-berth sea-going yacht which we keep at Hunter's Quay—on the Isle of Bute.'

'Very nice—but very expensive.'

'So we hire it out to make it earn its keep.'

'I've never done any deep-water sailing,' said Lucy half enviously.

'Then come with us some time,' Iain invited.

'I wasn't fishing,' she protested.

'I was,' he returned positively. 'Most of the girls I know get seasick before we reach the Cloch lighthouse, never mind Ailsa Craig.'

'So that's why. . .' Lucy stopped.

'Go on,' he urged. 'You may as well. I could tell it wasn't going to be a compliment.'

'All right, then. I have heard it said that you change your girlfriends as often as you. . .you——'

'Change my socks? Not quite. And good seamanship is not the main criterion for the post—just the icing on the cake.'

'Have you thought of advertising?' Lucy asked pertly. 'That could save time and disappointment for both parties.'

'If you turn out to be not quite what I'm looking for, I may do just that,' retorted Iain. Which, not surprisingly, left her without an answer.

She pretended to be absorbed in the scenery which, though a pleasing enough prospect of fields, trees and neat wayside cottages, was hardly the best which Scotland had to offer. Iain saw through her ruse, as evinced by the humorous curve of his mouth. It was quite a relief when they reached Balloch.

The basin was packed solid with sailing dinghies of all sizes. And so near to the loch, a breeze was stirring. The air was full of the metallic slap-slap of rigging against masts—rivalled only by the screaming of gulls circling overhead. 'How does anybody ever find their own boat—and get it away?' wondered Lucy.

'More by luck than judgement,' Iain considered. 'Which is why I keep mine moored in the bay around the corner in summer.'

Wouldn't you know it? she thought. The man thinks of everything!

They drove on, and when some minutes later Iain parked by the shore and got out, Lucy ran eagerly round to join him. 'Which one is your boat?' He pointed to a sleek blue-hulled craft dipping lazily at her moorings. 'Oh Iain! She's beautiful!' she exclaimed.

Lucy had never called him by his first name before, and his firm lips were twitching as he said, 'I'm so glad you approve.' He took lifejackets from the boot of the car and tossed one to Lucy before leading the way down a rickety wooden landing stage to an inflatable rubber dinghy.

'I suppose this is a communal boat,' observed Lucy, stepping nimbly in.

'No—mine. The old chap who does odd jobs around the place brings her in for me when he knows I'm coming.'

'He thinks of everything.' This time she had said it aloud. With approval.

'Your attitude has taken a definite upturn since you clapped those big blue eyes on my boat,' he considered.

'With some girls it's cars. But with me, it's definitely boats,' she explained.

He let that pass, to assume, 'You'll not have got much sailing down south.'

'Two hours now and again, in a tiny dinghy, on a flooded gravel pit. If I was lucky,' she added.

'No wonder you decided to emigrate,' he sympathised in heartfelt accents as they reached *Aurora*.

'Now then,' he continued, once they were aboard, had hitched the dinghy astern and were ready to cast off, 'I think we should do a circuit of the bay to let you get the feel of things.'

But it didn't take long for him to decide that Lucy was competent. 'You're no beginner,' he said by way of praise. 'How about running round that island there, and then cutting across to Luss for lunch?'

'Perfect!' Apart from anything else, Luss was on the opposite side of Loch Lomond from home. And Jock spent many nostalgic hours watching the boats through his binoculars. And Lucy hadn't confessed yet.

Away from the shore, the breeze was stiffer, the water choppier and the necessary changes of tack had to be carried out more quickly. But no problems. 'It's as though we'd been sailing together for years,' observed Iain with deep satisfaction. 'Would you like to take the tiller for a bit, Lucy?'

'Oh, thank you, Iain, I'd love that,' she answered eagerly. What further proof of approval could he have given?

The loch was crossed without mishap and landfall made exactly where Iain had directed. 'They've certainly spruced this place up since I was here last,' noticed Lucy when they had dropped anchor and gone ashore in the dinghy. 'Are you sure they still take in watery wayfarers like us?'

He chuckled at her description and laid a friendly arm across her shoulders for the stroll over the springy turf to the hotel. 'They'd better—especially as I fixed up the proprietor when he fractured his humerus last summer. Now then—in or out?'

'To eat? Oh, outside, most definitely.' Lucy pointed to the marquee coming into view on the leeward side of the building. 'It looks as if there's a function of some sort in progress.'

'A wedding, most probably,' Iain said scornfully. Into Lucy's head came the memory of an old saying of her grandmother's; something about he who holds out longest falling hardest in the end. Iain was saying, 'If you want to powder your nose, I'll get you a drink and find us a table on the terrace.'

Very tactful! 'Darn it,' she said brightly, 'if I haven't gone and forgotten my powder puff! I could do with washing my hands, though.' She held out a pair of very grubby paws, palms upwards.

'Ditto,' he laughed appreciatively. 'See you in five minutes, then.'

But the ladies' room was full of wedding guests dressed up to the nines, so it was longer than that before Lucy rejoined Iain. 'I got mixed up with that wedding party,' she explained.

'So did I—and they were very careful to keep their hired morning coats well away from my more functional costume!'

'And I wasn't too popular among the silks and laces either.'

Iain grinned at her over the rim of his glass. 'So here's to us—the peasantry.' He leaned forward and asked a trifle anxiously, 'Perhaps you'd rather have had something other than that lime and ginger concoction.'

'I'm flattered that you remembered how much I like it.'

'I went ahead and ordered two lobster salads too. That seemed appropriate for a day afloat.'

'Perfect,' Lucy assured him.

'That's the second time you've said that this morning.'

'Go on as you are doing, and I'll very likely say it again,' promised Lucy, having by now quite forgotten that she was supposed to have reservations about this man.

'Here's to the next time, then,' said Iain, promptly raising his glass for another toast.

By the time they had finished their drinks, the bride and groom had arrived for their reception. They looked so young; neither of them could be more than twenty-one, realised Lucy, feeling quite old as she watched them walking radiantly hand-in-hand across the grass to the marquee. 'Happy ever after, my children,' she breathed.

Iain made a very derisory noise. 'To the triumph of

hope over proof positive to the contrary would be more appropriate.'

Lucy frowned at him. 'I was only wishing them what they must surely be wishing for themselves.'

Cynicism distorted his mouth. 'Of course they are—now. But the fact remains that one in three marriages ends in divorce nowadays.'

'There's nothing new about divorce,' Lucy answered quietly. 'My own parents divorced when I was very young.'

'Really?' Eyes alight with interest, he leaned towards her, his arms folded on the roughly hewn table-top. 'So did mine. And it's not much fun for the bairns, is it?' They shared a look of silent understanding before he added heavily, 'Just the sort of thing to put them off the so-called state of bliss, when they grow up.'

'It certainly makes one think very carefully.'

'Is that why——?'

'Partly—though more because I haven't met any man worth making the supreme sacrifice for.'

Their salads arrived, and Iain sat back in his chair again. 'That's a very odd phrase to use in connection with marriage. I thought it was still every girl's goal—except for the hard-bitten careerists.'

'I'm not sure that marriage is such a big deal,' Lucy returned slowly. 'Especially nowadays when it's so common for a man to trade in his wife for a younger model every so often.'

'That may have been what your father did, but in my case, it was my mother who bolted,' Iain said bitterly.

'I'm sorry,' Lucy sympathised gently. 'My parents parted by mutual consent, so I guess I was luckier than you in that.'

Silence for a while as they ate—and then Iain said experimentally, 'There are alternatives to marriage.'

'You mean affairs,' realised Lucy. 'But like everything else in this male-orientated world they too are slanted largely in favour of men.'

'Are you a feminist, then?' he asked, frowning.

'Heaven forbid! No, I'm just a realist.' For a day of pleasure, she thought, this conversation was getting a bit too deep. 'That's when I'm not daydreaming about Prince Charming riding up on his snow-white charger and carrying me off to his castle, you understand.' She added with a tiny smile.

'Or a blond Viking type with an Adam mansion and a half-share in Fort Knox,' he reminded her. They stared at one another again until laughter bubbled up to the surface, lightening the mood and dispersing the tension.

'What would you like for dessert?' asked Iain when not a morsel of lobster remained.

'Thanks, Iain, but I couldn't possibly eat any more!'

'Nonsense! I'm going to work you really hard this afternoon, so you'll need the fuel. How about some apple pie? Or would you rather have the gâteau?'

'If you're insisting, then may I have some fruit salad, please?'

'Not many calories in that, but if it's what you want. . .' He ordered it, plus some apple pie for himself and two coffees. Then he stood up. 'And while we're waiting, I'll just go down to the dinghy and get the water bottle.'

Lucy watched him stride easily across the grass to the shore, athletic and graceful as a panther. And she wasn't the only woman watching him either. She remembered Tom saying that Iain was too attractive for his own good and that the lassies wouldn't leave him alone. Well, here was one who had better if she knew what was good for her. Lucy sighed. Why did life have to be so complicated?

Iain and the waiter arrived back at the table together, and when Iain had asked him to get their water bottle filled, Lucy asked why they needed water.

Iain dropped into his chair and grinned at her. 'Because we might put in somewhere and make tea.'

'Aren't we going straight back to Balloch, then?' she asked.

'In June—and with such long light? Heavens, no!'

'The forecast was for freshening winds and rain.'

'Which so far haven't materialised. I do hope you're not turning out to be a fair-weather sailor, Lucy.'

'Certainly not!' she returned indignantly.

'Good, because I was thinking we should go to the head of the loch and back.'

'Lovely!'

He cocked a reproachful eyebrow. 'But not perfect?'

'Hang it all, then—why not?' she amended, laughing.

And it was perfect—or very nearly. At first. Beating up the loch with a light breeze ruffling their hair and tempering the heat of the day, then putting ashore in the late afternoon on a tiny island Lucy had never visited before.

'We'll swim and then dry off in the sun,' Iain promised gleefully as he threw the anchor overboard.

'That sounds idyllic, but I can think of one tiny flaw.'

'Like what?'

'Like I've not brought my bikini and I'm not sold on swimming in the nude.'

'Fear not. As an ex-Boy Scout I'm always prepared for any eventuality,' he assured her.

I'll bet you are, thought Lucy, unsure whether that tiny dance of her sensory nerves was due to anticipation or alarm.

Iain took a strong canvas bag out of the locker and dropped it into the dinghy. When they beached on the pebbly shore, he handed her a small pink bundle. 'My sister's,' he explained casually.

Lucy unrolled a very brief swimsuit, thinking, that's a likely story! 'Your sister has a most elegant figure,' she observed satirically.

'It's not too bad for the mother of twins. Look there's a nice big gorse bush over there which should adequately screen the most old-fashioned of girls.' As he was already taking off his shorts, Lucy went.

When she came back, Iain was in the water, swimming with the speed and ease of a seal. She'd been right that first day to guess that he would do a thing well or not at all. Another deplorable little *frisson* of pleasure. Lucy Trent, where are your morals? Apart from anything else, this man hates your mother, remember.

He waved to her and shouted, 'Come on in! It's not cold.'

What a pity! A cold dowsing might have been good for both of them, if his thoughts were anything like hers. Lucy ran into the water, dived under, and came up gasping. 'How could you say that? It's freezing!'

He came at her fast under water and pulled her down—rolling, surfacing, teasing and playful, like puppies or young otters. But ten minutes of that crystal-clear but icy water was enough even for him, and they headed for shore to lie on the soft, warm grass and soak up the sun.

Still lying on her stomach, Lucy turned her head and squinted at Iain, stretched full length on his back. His splendidly muscled body was evenly tanned. How many other Saturdays had it taken to achieve that tan? And with how many other girls stretched out beside him in this same pink swimsuit? When he reached out towards her, as she'd been sure he would, Lucy rolled over out of range. 'This is bound to be a silly question,' she supposed, 'but just how are we going to make tea?'

He didn't open his eyes to explain lazily, 'On a brushwood fire, of course. There's plenty of it lying around.' He reached and felt for her again.

Lucy sat up. 'I'll start collecting, then,' she said briskly.

'Are you dry?'

She stood up. 'Would you believe not even still wet behind the ears?' His laughter followed her up the slope and into the tiny wood that crowned the island.

By the time Lucy returned, Iain had built a rectangle of stones and filled the kettle. 'Is that stuff quite dry, Lucy?' he asked.

'As dry as I could find.'

'It'll do—especially with this.' Having felt the bundle, he reached into the canvas bag and brought out a bottle of methylated spirit.

Lucy squatted down on the ground. 'This is fascinating,' she said. 'What else have you got in your magician's bag?'

'Everything that's needed.' He threw a match on the fire, which flared up at once as she had known it would.

'When Jock and I went picnicking, our fires never did more than smoke us like kippers,' she remembered unguardedly.

'And who's Jock?' Iain pounced.

'J-just a friend.' It might have been too good a lead to say 'my grandfather', when Jock had twice been president of the local branch of the BMA.

'You must be cold—your teeth are chattering!' exclaimed Iain, snatching up his sweater and draping it round her shoulders.

'Thank you—how thoughtful you are.' But Lucy was

thinking that last time she'd stammered, he'd blamed it on Maggie. . .

'Past or present?' he queried.

She looked at him, puzzled. 'Sorry?'

'This Jock. Is he still on the scene?'

'We don't—don't go out together any more.' Not with the old darling crippled the way he was now.

'That's all I wanted to know,' he said. The kettle boiled and he made the tea, handing her a steaming mug.

'That was quick,' Lucy remarked.

'When I decide to do something, no matter how simple, I don't hang about.'

'I've noticed.'

The tea was quite passable, despite the UHT milk, and Iain had even brought biscuits. But by the time they had finished their picnic, the breeze had quickened to a keen wind and clouds were billowing up from the west. Iain squinted up at the sky. 'So we're to get that weather after all. It'll be a lively trip back, I'm thinking.' It was a prospect he was clearly relishing. 'Away behind your pumpkin, then, Cinders, and get into your clothes before the rain comes on.'

They were hit by a squall while securing the dinghy. Lucy wasn't frightened. She'd been out in this sort of thing before and she knew she was with an experienced and able sailor. All the same, they were twenty slow and watery miles from Balloch, and even with oilskins they would be cold and probably damp by the time they got there. But *Aurora* was a splendid boat and she handled superbly.

The rain was easing off by the time they reached the foot of the loch. Even so, it was surprising to see a small cluster of people on the shore away to starboard. They were waving and shouting. 'Good grief—what a day to stand and watch the boats!' cried Lucy over her shoulder to Iain.

'Away back tae yer bus, ye daft keelies!' was Iain's reaction until something on the port bow caught his attention. 'Oh, my God!' he exclaimed, throwing the helm hard over.

Lucy responded by instinct, trimming the sails. To a thin cheer from the shore, they ran before the wind on the altered tack. Having by now complete faith in Iain's judgement, Lucy hadn't questioned his abrupt change of course. And she didn't grasp the reason for it until they reached a tiny inflatable boat with a child clinging to it. Big waves were washing over him, and in the instant she spotted him, he lost his grip and with a weak, despairing cry, slipped beneath the water.

'Hold her steady!' Iain had stripped off his oilskins and kicked off his shoes. He dived in.

Lucy fought to control both tiller and sails, while racked with anxiety for Iain and the child. Iain surfaced and looked round, treading water. There was no sign of the boy. Iain headed for the toy boat in the instant the child bobbed up behind him.

'Behind you!' shrieked Lucy, but the wind whipped away her cry. Just as the child sank again, Iain turned. Had he seen him? He had dived. . .

When a hand gripped the boat's side, Lucy crouched to help. Together they hoisted the child over the gunwale into the wildly veering craft. Then somehow Lucy got *Aurora* under control again as Iain climbed aboard. 'Beach her!' he ordered, rolling the child prone and starting to pump the water out of his lungs.

'But the hull. . .'

'Damn the hull—this is an emergency!'

Lucy headed for the shore and the watching crowd, speeded there by the following wind. *Aurora* struck bottom with a sickening crash and listed over. People splashed into the water to help carry the boy ashore. But when they looked like taking him to the waiting bus, Iain roared, 'Put him down!' He dropped to his knees beside the child. 'God, Lucy—he's arrested!'

He struck the child's chest a violent blow and a woman screeched hysterically, 'Stop that, ye bastard! He's a good lad!'

Iain ignored her and began cardiac massage. Lucy seized the nearest man. 'Get an ambulance—quickly! Go!' Then she too sank down on the pebbly beach.

'Mouth-to-mouth, Lucy!'

'Sure!'

Aterwards, Lucy couldn't have told how long they worked, but she sensed that Iain was on the point of giving up when he felt a faintly fluttering pulse. He redoubled his efforts, ordering Lucy to keep it going.

And still the ambulance hadn't come. Had that stupid man understood?

'Could we not take him to hospital in the bus, mister?' suggested somebody.

'Quite impractical,' Iain answered tersely as at last the first faint sounds of a siren came out of the distance; a sound never more welcome in life.

Two figures in navy blue came thrusting through the crowd, carrying a stretcher. One of them recognised Iain. 'Why, Mr Lennox! Lucky you were here, sir.'

'You could say that.' Rapidly, concisely, Iain gave details and instructions. Breathing apparatus was fixed in place and the child was on his way, his frantic mother with him.

Iain bent down to help an exhausted Lucy to her feet. 'Let's get out of here—we've still got the dinghy,' he whispered. But with the crisis now over, they were hemmed in by a crowd eager to congratulate them.

Iain put his arm around Lucy and pushed through the throng. 'Thanks, you're very kind. only too glad to help. Must see to the boat. . .'

*Aurora* was of course quite unseaworthy. With the briefest of sorrowful glances, Iain helped Lucy into the dinghy, transferred their belongings and cut loose. As the outboard motor spluttered into life, two uniformed figures wearing caps with checked bands could be seen running down the beach. The police had arrived.

'Just in time,' breathed Iain.

The rain was lashing down again, but they weren't very far from the landing stage and from there, it was but a few steps to Iain's car. Reaching it, they sank gratefully into their seats. 'Thank goodness we got away!' breathed Lucy. 'Imagine having to go over it all again— giving our names—even getting into the papers, perhaps. Ugh!'

'There are people who yearn to get into the papers,' said Iain.

'I know—isn't it incredible?' Lucy turned to him, her eyes alight with admiration. 'You were absolutely marvellous! The way you dived in and found him when he kept going under. . .'

'Havers! Who kept the boat from capsizing?'

'And then wrecked it!'

'You were only carrying out orders——' Iain sneezed violently.

Lucy felt his shirt. 'Oh dear, you're soaked,' she breathed worriedly. 'Maybe we should have waited for the police after all. They might have been able to help with dry clothing and a hot drink!'

'Dinnae fret, hen.' He hadn't turned the car, but was driving on down the bumpy track. 'I can rustle up both in about five minutes—at my weekend retreat.' He took a quick look to see how that had gone down.

'I should have known you knew exactly what you were doing,' said Lucy.

'Somebody is definitely in a state of shock,' Iain considered humorously as he brought the car to a halt beside a sturdy log cabin in a small woodland encampment. They hurried inside.

The cabin felt quite warm, but Iain switched on the electric fire. 'A hot drink while the water heats up,' he decided going to fill a kettle in the tiny open-plan kitchen. He returned to strip off Lucy's oilskins and throw them into a corner. 'Your clothes are damp and you're shivering,' he discovered with concern.

'I'm not cold—it's just. . .' Her face crumpled and she began to cry. 'Oh, Iain! Will he die?' she sobbed.

He pulled her against him, regardless of his sodden clothing, and held her close, stroking her hair. 'I don't know, honey. But at least we did all that could be done. Hold on to that.' When the kettle boiled with a splutter and a hiss, he eased her gently into a chair close to the fire and went to make cocoa. That done, he folded her hands round a mug of it. 'Drink this—you'll feel better when you're warm.' Then he squatted on the hearthrug at her feet, and in no time, his clothes were steaming gently in the heat from the fire.

Seeing that, Lucy forgot her anxiety about the boy. 'You must get out of those wet things at once,' she commanded.

'Are you suggesting that I do a striptease?' he asked, glad to note the beginning of a smile on her anxious face. 'Don't fret, hen—another quarter of an hour'll not kill me. So finish your drink, have a hot shower and I guarantee you'll be a new woman. Not that there's a lot wrong with the old one,' he added under his breath.

'I'm not going first—you are,' Lucy insisted. 'Do you want to get pneumonia?'

'I hope it'll take more than a dip in Loch Lomond to achieve that.' An ill-timed sneeze rather undermined his argument.

'There, what did I say? I mean it, Iain. I'm not moving from this chair until you're warm and dry.'

'We could always shower together,' he said slyly. 'What do you think of that for a compromise?' Another gigantic sneeze.

'Not a lot,' said Lucy. 'One more sneeze like that, in a confined space, and I'd be infected too. Now will you *please* go and get dry? You're worrying me.'

'The woman's inexorable!' he sighed, getting to his feet to fetch dry clothes from an adjoining room. He dropped a large towelling bathrobe on Lucy's knees. 'Strip off your wet things and get into that while I'm in the shower, do you hear? You're not the only one who can give orders.' He strode across the cabin, pausing at the shower-room door to say thoughtfully, 'When you came over all bossy just now, you reminded me of somebody, but I'm damned if I can think who it is.' He went in and shut the door. Almost at once came the sound of running water and some rather nice bass singing.

Lucy shivered and crept nearer to the fire. So much had happened that day that she had quite forgotten his feud with her mother, until reminded. For who could he have meant but Maggie? It couldn't be long before he found out and then it would be curtains. Resolutely, she faced the fact that that was the last thing she wanted— now. Yet how else could it be? Iain might be able to accept having her as a colleague, but Maggie Fearnan's daughter for a girlfriend? That he would never tolerate. I mustn't get any closer to him, she realised.

As the warmth gradually seeped into her weary bones, Lucy looked round the cabin. Just the bare minimum, but comfortable. Armchairs around the fire, a huge and fluffy hearthrug, books, a television set, and, over by the half wall, separating the main room from the tiny kitchen, a pine table and benches. Presumably, a bedroom lay beyond that half-open door. Everything that the weekend yachtsman could require. Except that the owner of this comfortable base no longer had a yacht.

Knowing that waiting to anchor *Aurora* safely and then taking the child ashore in the dinghy would lose vital minutes, Iain had unhesitatingly destroyed his most prized possession. Impossible not to feel a strong surge of admiration for the man who could do that. Who could have foreseen that a single day would be long enough to add respect and admiration to an already strong attraction? In any other circumstances. . .

Lucy had been too engrossed in her thoughts to hear Iain approaching barefoot over the cork-tiled floor. 'You're a fine one to be handing out lectures—you haven't even changed,' he said, causing her to jump.

She looked up at him. He was dressed now in trousers and an old checked shirt, and his bright hair was still damp—thus curling more tightly than ever. He reached down and hauled her to her feet. He filled her arms with the bathrobe and some towels, then turning her round, he sent her off to shower with a firm pat on the bottom. To his obvious surprise, Lucy went without a word of protest.

When she returned to the living-room, she saw that the table was set for a meal and Iain was opening a jar of peaches in brandy. 'Don't look so surprised,' he said. 'It's way past dinnertime.'

A glance at the clock confirmed that. 'You're very well organised,' she realised, after giving the kitchen a closer look and noting both a fridge-freezer and a microwave oven among all the units.

'And why not? I spend nearly all my free weekends here.'

Alone—or in company? None of your business, Lucy. This is the terminus for you.

The timer intervened and Iain took plates of food out of the microwave. 'Chicken Kiev,' he said. 'And if you don't like it, then too bad, because it's all there is. The freezer is due for restocking.'

'Perfect,' she said, sitting down at the table. At that they exchanged glances, remembering all the times she'd said that earlier in the day. Iain's eyes were warm and eager, but Lucy looked away quickly, afraid to respond. So she missed his subsequent look of disappointment.

The simple meal over and the few dishes washed and put away, Iain made coffee before switching on the television. 'Just in time for the tail end of the news. You never know—there may be something about our little adventure.'

There was—and rather more than they had bargained for. 'And now finally, news of a dramatic rescue,' promised the announcer. 'A boy aged nine was rescued from Loch Lomond earlier this evening, when his pleasure boat capsized in a sudden squall.' Iain snorted at the grandiose description of the lethal little craft. 'His rescuer was Mr Iain Lennox, a consultant surgeon at the Glasgow General Hospital.' Gasps from them both. 'Mr Lennox and his female companion, who were passing in their yacht, pulled the boy from the water and then successfully revived him with the kiss of life. The boy, named as Gavin McCluskey of Easterhouse, is now stable in the Intensive Care Unit at Glasgow's Northern General Hospital. Now after the Evening Call——'

'Hell and damnation!' growled Iain, reaching out and switching off the set.

'The ambulance man!' wailed Lucy.

'Who else? And you can guess what this means.'

'Reporters on your doorstep?'

'Precisely.' He sighed heavily.

'But you'll be very late getting home, so they might get tired and go away.'

'Not while there's a chance of getting a column in tomorrow's late editions.' Iain sent Lucy a level look across the hearthrug. 'Fortunately, this is the sort of incident which usually rates no more than twenty-four hours of news coverage. . .' A pause for Lucy to digest that. 'So staying up here tonight would seem to be the best way of avoiding any more publicity.'

'Ah—um.' Feeble, but the best Lucy could come up with, faced with that suggestion. She looked round the room. 'And where——?'

'There is a bedroom, so you're not expected to sleep on the floor. I'll do that.' The look he gave her was quizzical. Was he expecting her to tell him that wouldn't be necessary?

A vigorous knocking on the door saved Lucy from having to answer. Iain got to his feet with an exclamation of impatience. 'One of the neighbours wanting to borrow something,' he surmised. 'They come up here on impulse and without stocking up——' He had opened the door and was frowning out into the rain-washed near-darkness. 'Yes? What can I do for you?'

'Just a word, Mr Lennox. Y'see, when we found you weren't at your Glasgow address, we rang the Yacht Club in Balloch—just on the off chance that you were a member.' It was clear that whoever was out there thought he deserved a pat on the back for being so resourceful. 'And by good luck, somebody had spotted your car outside your cabin.'

The police was Lucy's thought as Iain asked, 'And

what's so urgent that you had to track me all the way up here?'

No need to antagonise them, Iain. They're only doing their job. . .

'We're from the *Sunday Clarion*, Mr Lennox, and we'd like you to tell us in your own words all about the rescue of little Gavin McCluskey.'

No! Not that rag— the sleaziest of all the gutter press! And me still wearing Iain's bathrobe! Lucy leapt towards the bedroom door to hide, but she was too late. The reporter had ducked under Iain's arm—outstretched to bar entry—and had witnessed her attempted flight with great interest. He lifted his head like a bloodhound scenting prey. 'Well, well, well! The young lady in the case, if I'm not mistaken!'

After that, there was nothing for it but to let in the wretched man and his sidekick, and tell their story as briefly as possible—though without any hope that it would be printed in its simple, unvarnished state. 'As you can imagine, we were both soaked to the skin,' Iain concluded. 'So it was very fortunate that I have this place where we were able to dry our clothes and get hot drinks.' He stretched out to feel Lucy's shorts, draped over an airer before the fire. 'Still a bit damp, but you'll be able to get dressed soon, and then we can leave.'

He had handled the whole thing so well, but before Lucy had finished admiring such presence of mind the reporter said unctuously, 'Now then, if we could just have a picture of you and Miss Trent. Put your arm round her shoulders, sir—and you, dear, smile up at him like——'

At that Iain stepped in front of Lucy, effectively screening her. 'Right, that's it!' he exploded. 'I consider we've given you quite enough of our time. You've got your story—now kindly leave!'

All along gushing and somehow suggestive, the reporter abruptly switched off his smile. 'There's no need to get nasty, Mr Lennox. If you and the young lady don't care to be photographed together, I'm sure it's no business of ours. Come on, Sandy. Pity about your pic, but we've got more than enough material here!' That had sounded very sinister.

Iain hustled them out and slammed the door after them. Then he rested his head against it in a gesture of frustration. 'God, Lucy, I'm so sorry I reacted like that. Heaven knows what they'll print now!'

'What they would have anyway—their own garish version,' she returned robustly, in spite of her own inner fears. 'So what? Nobody really believes the tripe they print.' Who was she trying to convince?

She certainly hadn't convinced Iain. 'Which is presumably why they have the largest circulation of any Sunday newspaper in Britain,' he returned satirically. 'The patients will give us some welcome on Monday!' They regarded each other in silent horror while visualising that—then Iain said wearily, 'Come on, let's go back to Glasgow. There's nothing to be gained by staying here now.'

They spoke little on the homeward journey, and then only to comment on the surprising amount of traffic for the time of day, and the fact that the rain had stopped at last. The closeness of the day was gone, dissolved by that reporter and the distorted, sordid picture he would most certainly contrive to paint.

As they turned into the drive of Lucy's apartment block, Iain said in a tired voice, 'I've been thinking that we'd have been better to wait and speak to the police after all. If those tripehounds have also got hold of the fact that we dashed off so promptly——'

'Iain, don't! Anyway, surely people who know us will

be prepared to admit we were just being modest? Anyway, how could we know we were going to be hunted down? We did what seemed sensible at the time. How were we to know what would happen?'

'We weren't.' He stopped the car by the front entrance. 'Try to see it this way, Lucy. A day or two—a week at the most—and it will all have blown over.' He's angry and he's embarrassed, she decided unhappily.

'Yes, of course it will.' She paused. 'This is where I should thank you very much for a lovely day. Which it was until—oh, hell!'

'My sentiments exactly,' he agreed with a hollow laugh.

He got out of the car to get her holdall out of the boot. Lucy got out too, and took it from him. 'Well then——' she began uncertainly.

Iain reached out and pulled her towards him. 'What a damnable way for such a promising day to end,' he muttered, before kissing her just once with a sad and angry passion. Then he got back in his car and drove away.

Lucy watched him go, her hand to the cheek he had kissed in what she suspected was a final farewell. A day that had begun so well had ended in ruins. Since that reporter came, Iain had been withdrawn and preoccupied. Was he concerned and angry at the idea of publicity in general—or only because he had been found in compromising circumstances with the latest addition to his team?

# CHAPTER SIX

IN ORDER to sneak in unnoticed and avoid the crowd,
Lucy had arrived at the hospital very early. Now she
found herself sitting in her car, trying to pluck up the
courage to get out. Of all the daft, weak-kneed, spineless
creatures——Where's your courage, Lucy? she thought.
But she went on sitting there.

She had spent the previous day at the cottage, having
bought most of the Sunday papers on the way. Only one
named her as well as Iain, and all reported the rescue
factually. So far, so good. But she had deliberately saved
the *Clarion* until last, and she opened it with a thrill of
apprehension.

Her spirits sank; the *Clarion* had done its usual hatchet
job on their reputations. Without actually spelling it out,
that wretched reporter had contrived to give the clear
impression that he and his photographer had stumbled
on a scene of questionable morality. 'Miss Trent, clad
only in a dressing-gown. . . Mr Lennox, edgy and
embarrassed throughout the interview. . . Our reporters
insulted and forcibly ejected for asking politely if they
could take a photograph of the couple. . .'

However had they managed to make such a phrase as
'the couple' sound disgraceful? But—forcibly ejected?
Surely Iain could sue them for that. He hadn't laid a
finger on either of them, despite the provocation.

It would be hell at the hospital tomorrow, but first she
had to face her family. Netta had gone to see her sister
as she did every Sunday that Maggie was off duty. And
as Jock was in the garden, pottering about among his

roses, only Maggie was there. In dressing-gown and
slippers, a cigarette dangling from the corner of her
mouth, she sat at the kitchen table, reading the *Sunday
Times*. That was the only Sunday paper they took, and
there wouldn't be an account of the rescue in that.

Greetings over, Lucy asked as casually as possible if
Ma had happened to hear about yesterday's dramatic
rescue from the loch.

Maggie had then said, Yes, wasn't it fantastic? Iain
Lennox might be a chauvinist of the worst possible sort,
but he could always be relied upon to turn up trumps in
a crisis.

'He did have—some help,' Lucy had pointed out by
way of leading up to her confession.

'You're referring to the female companion.' Maggie
had obviously got her information from last night's
bulletin on Scottish Television. 'Another poor deluded
girl in a long line of hopefuls, I guess. I wonder if that
lad will ever settle down?'

Not the most helpful of comments in the circumstances. Lucy had hummed and haaed and gone scarlet
before finally getting out in a strangled voice, 'It—she—
was me!' She had then stood staring down at her feet as
she waited for the skies to fall.

There followed a long moment of astounded silence
before Maggie let out a great guffaw, rolling about in her
chair and laughing till she cried. Then she got up and
slapped her daughter on the back. 'If that doesn't beat
all! I'd give a year's salary to see his face when he finds
out he's been chatting up my daughter. You did it,
Luce! You got round him—and how! So quickly too.'
Maggie paused to consider. 'Of course, it would be
awkward if he got serious about you—but I'm sure you
could handle it.'

Lucy had found herself strongly resenting her mother's conviction that mutual seriousness just wasn't a possibility. Stifling a sigh, she had said, 'Don't worry, Ma—he won't even want to look at me again after reading this.' She took the *Clarion* out of her holdall and handed it to her mother. 'We were soaked to the skin and only went to that cabin to get dry,' she said defensively as soon as Maggie had fumed her way through the account.

'Good God, girl, you don't have to tell *me* that—but this cannot go unchallenged.' Maggie stormed and swore for another minute or so before exclaiming, 'Of course! Dougie Fearnan'll soon sort that rag.' Maggie's nephew was a staff columnist on the *Glasgow Banner* who had waged more than one campaign against gutter journalism. 'I'm going to ring him now.'

'He won't be up yet,' returned Lucy, who knew her cousin.

'Then it's high time he was,' his aunt called over her shoulder.

Dougie, once fully conscious and suitably incensed, had promised to do whatever he could. Then, after agreeing that come what may, Jock must not be upset, Lucy and her mother had settled more or less easily into their usual off-duty Sunday routine, although the problem was ever present in Lucy's mind. Endlessly considering Iain's likely reactions, she had spent a restless night at the cottage and set off for Glasgow very early this morning.

And now here she was in the hospital car park, trying to pluck up courage to go in and face the music. Already it was eight o'clock, and the advantage of arriving early would be lost if she didn't move soon. With a great effort, Lucy got out of her car and made for the entrance at a pace more suited to a day of wind and rain than to this one of cloudless sunshine.

'Emergency,' speculated one porter to another as she whizzed by them. Thus are rumours spread.

The first person Lucy saw on the unit that morning was Essie. 'Quick! In here!' she hissed, seizing Lucy's arm and hauling her into the privacy of the broom cupboard. 'Anybody can see that you didn't sleep much last night—and no wonder! But don't worry; Sister's taken care of things.'

She hadn't needed to tell Lucy what she meant. 'Don't tell me those ruddy reporters came here!' sighed Lucy.

'I don't know about that, but I do know that Kevin and Co. were all agog yesterday after they'd passed round that filthy scandal sheet.'

'How am I ever going to face them, Essie?' groaned Lucy.

'Am I not trying to tell you? Sister's off today, but she gave them all a right good telling off for so much as wondering if that rubbish was true—and Charge Nurse Kynoch is back from his holiday today, so he's going to hover in the men's ward during the class, at least.' Essie gave Lucy a playful slap on the wrist. 'Fancy you going out with Iain Lennox and having such an adventure! When I saw Lois Baird at breakfast this morning, she was looking as if she could cheerfully burst an artery. I expect that was because she told me on Friday that he was taking *her* out somewhere next day.'

'What a mess!' sighed Lucy; an assessment with which Essie promptly and depressingly agreed.

'Just wanted to set your mind at rest,' she summed up, unaware of any irony. 'I think Charge Nurse is in the office now, if you want an update. I must dash—I'm supervising dressings today.'

This was the first time Lucy had met John Kynoch.

Like Sister, he exuded quiet authority, and she was reassured at the thought of having his support when she faced Kevin. When they had shaken hands, she said diffidently, 'I've just been talking to Essie—Staff Nurse Munro—about all the—the fuss.'

He shook his head sadly. 'It's come to something when two people cannot save the life of a third without being pilloried for it.' Then he pulled the Kardex towards him. 'Now then—to work. There was only one admission yesterday—an old lady found wandering and confused. She has a right Colles fracture, a fracture of right fibula and numerous cuts and bruises. She couldn't give a history and, as she had no identification, we had to keep her in. Her damaged hand is very swollen, so perhaps you could do the necessary some time today.'

'That I will. Any new chests, Mr Kynoch?' He shook his head, so Lucy squared her shoulders and said, 'Right, I'd better get started, then.'

'I take it you've already seen Mr Lennox?' Seeing Lucy's look of surprise, he asked, 'Did Essie not tell you? He was in at the crack of dawn and left a message saying that he wanted to see you as soon as you came in. He's in his consulting-room.' The phone rang and he picked it up. 'She's on her way down now, sir,' he said in answer, nodding to Lucy.

She hurried down to Outpatients. On the way, she met several people she knew and fancied they were eyeing her curiously, despite their friendly greetings. Outside Iain's room she hesitated for several nervous seconds before knocking timidly on the door and going in.

Iain stood by the window, his back view rigid and uncompromising. When he swung round his expression was dark, and it didn't lighten much when he saw Lucy. 'Where the hell were you all day yesterday?' he demanded. 'I must have rung you a dozen times!' That might have been reassuring—if he hadn't sounded so angry.

'I went out very early to—to visit my grandfather,' she told him. 'And then I decided to stay the night.'

'It didn't occur to you that I might want to see you— if only to discuss how best to deal with the filthy innuendoes in that damned newspaper? Or didn't you see it?'

'Oh, yes, I saw it; I bought the beastly thing on purpose. As to meeting—I never even thought of it.' Lucy lifted her head and stared him challengingly in the eye. 'Quite frankly, I'd come to the conclusion that you were so angry and embarrassed by the whole thing that you wouldn't want to see me in any other than strictly professional circumstances.' She fancied she could detect a slight relaxation in his stance. Her suspicions were right, then—and he was relieved that she seemed to have taken his point.

'Of course I was angry and embarrassed,' he said. 'And so were you. It's a damnable situation in which to find ourselves, but the only thing to do is to act as normally as possible. We must agree to dismiss the *Clarion* and its foul insinuations as just one more piece of its usual bad taste. Overreacting—letting people *know* we're embarrassed—will only fuel suspicions that we really have got something to hide. Surely you can see that?'

'Indeed I do see—and very clearly,' Lucy answered quietly. Oh, yes, she saw exactly what he was getting at!

He stared at her, as if he didn't quite know what to make of her answer. 'So we're in agreement, then, are we?' he asked.

'But of course! How could we not be?' A light and most convincing laugh went with that. 'And now I'd better get going. We can't risk somebody coming in and finding us alone together. That would certainly fuel suspicions.'

'I suppose so.' He had said that almost doubtfully, but then he could afford to be less emphatic, now that he had her agreement, couldn't he? Don't worry, Iain Lennox—Lucy doesn't run after men! 'I'll see you later on, then, Lucy,' he said in the same doubtful tone.

How much reassurance did he need, for heaven's sake? 'I don't see how you can avoid that,' she retorted with another well-contrived laugh, before going out and shutting the door.

She went over that scene again as she returned to Ortho. No doubts now about having read his reactions aright on Saturday night. He *had* been furious at being found in potentially compromising circumstances with a junior colleague, the very first time he took her out. And, even more importantly, before he had decided whether or not there was going to be a second time. There certainly wouldn't be now, as he had just made very clear. All that was needed now was for somebody to tell him she was Maggie Fearnan's daughter, and her day would be complete!

Back on the unit, Lucy went first to see yesterday's admission. Then she made sure that Mr Kynoch was in the men's ward before entering.

Her appearance was the signal for a chorus of good mornings. Nothing new about that—but then, with a wink for Mike Craig, Kevin asked, 'Did you have a nice weekend, Lucy?'

Lucy took a deep breath that was meant to be calming. 'Saturday was very exciting, as I'm sure you know from the television, but yesterday I spent with my family, and that was quite uneventful.'

'You havena' told us what ye did on Saturday night,' prompted Kevin, to the accompaniment of sniggers.

'I had intended going to a disco with—with my cousin,' Lucy invented, feeling very proud of such ingenuity. 'But rescuing people from drowning is very tiring, so I just stayed quietly at home—my home is on Loch Lomondside,' she added. She was throwing out too many clues, but now that she and Iain were finished it really didn't matter. What did matter was that she appeared to have outwitted Kevin—at least for the moment, as his expression clearly showed, so Lucy took advantage of that to get on with the class.

'You may have been tired on Saturday, but you're surely not tired the morn,' panted Mike Craig when she told them they could now stop stretching forward to touch their toes.

'Of course not! As I was telling Kevin earlier, yesterday was very peaceful, just helping my grandfather with the garden. Isn't it great that you've got your traction off? Now we'll be able to get that knee bending. I'll fetch you an exercise board like Mr Watson's and you two can have a race to see who gets full flexion first.'

With a smile and a nod, Charge Nurse Kynoch left the ward, satisfied that Lucy wouldn't need reinforcements.

'Miss Trent?'

'Yes, Mr Murray?'

'Mr Craig will be going to X-ray for a check any minute now, so if the film is satisfactory, could you get him up on crutches this afternoon?'

'It'll be a pleasure. And don't look so worried, Mr Craig—I never drop my patients unless they annoy me.' Lucy looked at Kevin as if to remind him where the power really lay.

'I shall tell your boyfriend what you said,' Kevin retaliated.

'That'll be difficult—he's abroad on business in—in Japan!' Lucy Trent, you're a wonder!

'Does he know you go out with other guys behind his back?'

'That depends on what you mean by that,' said Lucy calmly. More inspiration! 'You see, it's my boyfriend who usually crews for Mr Lennox and I was only standing in for him on Saturday.' Have I always been a good liar, then—or is this just the result of pressure? 'Now then, as you've still so much breath left, Kevin, I think I'll give you a heavier weight to lift today.'

How Kevin might have replied to that was to remain a mystery, because agitated calls from the other end of the ward had Lucy running to investigate.

One of last Thursday's meniscectomies was lying on the floor by his bed, having a fit. Send Mr Buchan hirpling down the ward to get help. No gag on the locker, so improvise one with a hankie wrapped round my lovely gold pencil. Get him prone with his head to one side. . .

Lucy stood up. 'I think he's coming out of it now, Mr Kynoch,' she said as the charge nurse came running up.

He took in the situation at a glance. 'There'll be some questions asked about this, I'm thinking, but well done, Miss Trent.'

'Just glad to be of use,' she said. Nobody had known he was an epileptic, then.

'Like you were on Saturday.' He turned round to face the ward. 'Miss Trent's a useful soul to have around in a crisis, isn't she, lads?'

A chorus of agreement, with Kevin unable to think of a remark, for once.

'That was a very good impression of Daley Thompson

you gave us, Mr Buchan,' said Lucy when calm was restored. 'I hope you're not too tired to do your exercises now. There's just time before the coffee comes round.'

'Charge Nurse tells me I've an appointment with the Limb Fitting Centre this afternoon.'

'Good, then we'd better measure that hip flexion contracture. They'll do it too, of course, but we wouldn't want them to think we're not on the ball.'

'Don't worry, hen—I'll tell them ye are. I've spent enough time lying on ma belly like a crocodile these past two weeks. Well?' Mr Buchan bent forward to squint at the goniometer.

'I make it fifteen degrees, which is nothing, practically speaking. Now all we have to do is to make sure the extensors and adductor muscles are really strong.'

'Why *is* that, hen?'

'Because some of each had to be severed, while the other groups were not. It depends where the muscles are attached, you see. If we didn't strengthen the cut muscles, you'd soon be out of kilter.'

'Out of kilter,' he repeated with a grin. 'You're picking up the Scots phrases fast! And thanks for the explanation.'

'I would have explained before, only——'

'You've been that busy—I ken. The way you girls in this hospital hirple about'd make a strong man go on strike!'

'I expect that's why we're all so thin,' smiled Lucy. 'Now then, I'm giving you a forty-pound spring today. Pull down hard and hold for a count of twenty before letting go. Very slowly. . .'

'I'm sorry I'm no' gettin' the magic box any more, Miss Trent.'

'You don't need it any more, Mr Govan. Not now the swelling's down. You'll be getting plasters put on now and then you'll not have to be in bed all the time.' Thank goodness he hadn't asked about walking. Having both heel bones fractured at the same time made that impossible. . .

'No, Mr Dodson, don't try to get around without your Zimmer. I'm glad your hip doesn't hurt, but it will if you put too much weight on it. . .'

'Miss Trent, you're wanted urgently. Come on!'

'I doubt the Queen's going to give ye a medal—for standin' in for your boyfriend,' suggested Kevin satirically as Lucy dashed out after Essie.

'Whatever's wrong?' she asked, catching up with her.

'Nothing—well, not really. It's STV. They've come to interview you and Mr Lennox.'

'In the middle of the morning?'

'It's not the middle of the morning—it's getting on for lunchtime.' Essie, always so precise. 'You'll find them in the car park.'

Looking out of the stair window as she went, Lucy saw a squat green van, festoons of cable and scurrying figures. A girl with great things like conch shells over her ears was talking to a white-coated figure, spelling disapproval in his every line. Please let this thing die a natural death very soon, prayed Lucy, speeding up, anxious to get the interview over.

When she got there, Iain acknowledged her with a curt nod. Lucy smiled back tentatively, and then pretended to take a great interest in all the paraphernalia. It wasn't the ordeal that the interview with the *Clarion* reporter had been. All the TV crew wanted was a straightforward account in their own words of the rescue and the resuscitation. Plus some questions. The girl with the conch shells thrust a thing that looked like a teazle under Iain's nose and gushed, 'How lucky for wee Gavin that two folk with the right expertise were on the spot!'

'Yes, Iain agreed impassively.

Lucy's turn. 'And what were your thoughts as you worked on the child, Miss Trask?'

Call me anything you like so long as it's not Ms Fearnan's daughter! thought Lucy. 'I'm not sure that I thought about anything, except getting it right. One just sort of goes into overdrive in a situation like that—and works instinctively.' Lucy glanced at Iain and he nodded in agreement.

His turn again. 'I'm sure you never expected a day's sailing to end up like that, Mr Lennox.'

Iain looked slightly dazed at being expected to comment on so fatuous a remark. 'I can honestly say that such a possibility never entered my mind,' he said.

'And you didn't hesitate to wreck your beautiful boat. How unselfish!'

'It was necessary—every second counted,' Iain returned matter-of-factly.

'So there'll be no sailing for you next weekend, then.' The teazle was under Lucy's nose again—and it was too good a chance to miss.

'I don't know about that—it really depends on whether anybody else is short of an assistant—as Mr Lennox was on Saturday. I don't have my own boat yet, you see.' There, Iain, I've done my best to get you off the hook.

'I'm sure you'll not be short of offers after your splendid seamanship last Saturday, Miss Troup.'

Good heavens, no! There must be hundreds of yachtsmen bursting to have me beach their precious boats, thought Lucy. But the girl was now speaking directly to the camera. 'This dramatic rescue has captured the imagination of all our viewers, and in response to many requests, STV is setting up a fund to replace Mr Lennox's boat. Contributions should be sent to——'

Iain tackled the producer standing calmly by, arms folded. 'You can't do that! If you must set up a fund, let it be for the boy.'

'Viewer power, squire,' was the laconic response, but Iain wasn't having that. He argued until he got his way—and a promise that the next bulletin would correct the impression just given. Then the producer asked, 'Is there a chance that you two could visit young Gavin in the Northern later on today? It would round off this little item very nicely.'

'Out of the question. I'm on call tonight.' Iain had endured all the publicity he intended to.

'I suppose tomorrow would do, but it'd have more impact tonight. How about you, dear?' the producer asked Lucy.

She hesitated. If she were to agree, would they then leave Iain alone? 'Well—at least I'm not on call. . .'

'Right, then. Be at the Northern by five and we can put it out on the early evening news.'

'Sorry, but half-six is quite the earliest I could manage.' Lucy gave the man her most dazzling smile. 'You wouldn't want me to neglect my patients, now, would you?'

So six-thirty was agreed on, and as the crew began to gather up their gear, Lucy looked round for Iain. But he had already gone. There's gratitude, she thought grimly, as she headed back towards the hospital. Ma's right about you. You're a selfish, self-centred, chauvinistic. . . A hand shot out and drew her into the lee of a parked minibus. 'You nearly gave me a heart attack, Iain Lennox!' Lucy accused breathlessly.

'Glad I didn't quite,' he returned briskly. 'I've had all the excitement of that sort I can handle for the moment.' His look, she noticed, was one of approval. 'You did very well just now.'

'Glad you approve. I thought that if only we could implant the idea that sailing together on Saturday was a—a sort of accident, rather than pre-planned. . .' She wasn't making her point too well.

The approval went out of his glance. 'I realise what you were trying to do there—but I was actually referring to the way you handled that fellow when fixing up tonight's interview. I'm sorry you got landed with that.'

'Don't be. With luck, that will be the end of—of the affair.' And she didn't just mean the matter of the rescue.

'It's lunchtime,' he said suddenly, with apparent irrelevance.

'Yes, and I'm supposed to be joining Sally Lawson in Physio for a sandwich and a bit of pre-planning.'

'Then please don't let me delay you,' Iain said sardonically.

Lucy looked at him in surprise, wondering what thoughts lay behind that impassive expression. 'But of course, if there was something important. . .' she offered.

'Something tells me that you wouldn't consider it so,' he returned crisply, before stalking off towards the canteen.

So had he only been making sure that she wasn't headed in the same direction? If so, it was all of a piece with his behaviour since that wretched reporter showed up on Saturday. Therefore, to be disappointed was stupid. Saturday wasn't the first time she'd been out once and once only with a man. What was so special about Mr High-and-Mighty Iain Lennox? Hurry along to the department, you silly goose, and get your mind back on your work! she told herself.

'Here she comes!'

'See the conquering heroine. . .'

'Tell us all about it, Lucy. Come on! Right from the beginning.'

'And we don't just mean the accident,' Sally Lawson underlined.

Lucy sighed. She'd half expected some such reaction from the other physios, but, having seen so little of them, she'd also half hoped to escape. 'Don't any of you read the *Clarion*?' she asked humorously. 'I can't improve on that.'

'That rag!'

'Ought to be banned!'

'Anyway, what has it got to do with saving a child's life if you *are* having an affair?' asked a striking redhead. Mhairi, the departmental siren, without a doubt. 'I wouldn't mind a little adventure with Iain Lennox myself.'

'Oh, Mhairi, haven't you got enough on your plate?' asked several people at once.

'Well, it was like this,' Lucy began. With repeated telling, it was getting easier to whittle it down to the barest facts and, as before, she contrived to give the impression that she and Iain had only teamed up on Saturday out of necessity; he needing a helper and she without a boat of her own. That story ought to hold as long as nobody thought of checking with his sailing club.

'Is that really all, then?' they chorused in disappointment.

Lucy chose to misunderstand. 'Sorry girls. If I do manage to get another sail, I'll try to arrange something a bit more spectacular—like a collison with the *Lady Fiona*,' she added, naming one of the most popular pleasure craft plying up and down Loch Lomond. She looked at Sally. 'If we're to have time for that chat. . .'

'Sure. We're staying here for a working lunch, girls, so don't wait for us.'

With the others off to the canteen, Lucy and Sally got down to essentials. 'You could really do with me up on the unit full time,' Sally realised afterwards.

'I know, but half a loaf is better than no bread.'

'Thank *you*,' returned Sally with a mock frown. 'It really is wonderful to be appreciated!'

First on the list was a visit for Mike Craig. He stared when he saw two physios approaching, having thought all he had to do was get up, grab his crutches and go. He didn't think much of his cast brace either. 'And how am I supposed to get ma jeans on over this thing?' he demanded.

'Sorry, lad,' said Lucy, 'but it's safety before fashion just now. Of course, if you've got a kilt, then——'

'And what kind of a daft jessie would I look on the buildin' site in ma kilt?'

'You'll not be going on the building site until you can discard the brace.'

'And when'll that be?'

'When the fracture is soundly healed.'

'Has Mr Lennox got a kilt, Lucy?' asked Kevin. Amazing that he'd managed to keep quiet for so long!

'I've no idea—you'll have to ask him yourself,' returned Lucy without looking up from the task of buckling on Mike's brace.

'Jest thocht he might have gone sailin' in it,' persisted Kevin.

Lucy elected to ignore such silliness. 'There we are then, Mr Craig, but gently does it. We'll get you upright and then you must stand for a minute or two, to clear your head. . .'

'It'll be much easier when we try again later on,' promised Sally when they returned Mike to his bed after a shaky half-length of the ward.

'I hope so. Hey! Whaur are ye goin' with ma crutches?'

'Just removing temptation,' explained Lucy. 'And don't you dare to put as much as a toe to the floor until we come back.'

'Some chance, with this damn' thing on ma leg!'

The girls had decided that it would be simpler if they each took a side in the women's ward. This left Lucy with most of the problems. Like Mrs Barr, who fancied she was going to the shops in Sauchiehall Street today. And Mrs Dorward, who was hanged if she was going anywhere. Lucy didn't argue, knowing it would be quite a different story about half an hour after her afternoon cuppa, when she'd be in dire need of a trip to the toilet. Every cloud has a silver lining, she thought, going next to Trisha.

'And how are ye the day, hen?' asked the patient, reversing roles, as she regarded Lucy with avid curiosity.

'As well as can be expected, thanks,' returned Lucy, playing up and hoping that was the end of that. She reached behind the radiator for Trish's exercise board.

'So you say, but I'll bet you've had a helluva day with the papers full o' you bein' found half undressed with Mr Lennox,' exaggerated Trisha with obvious sympathy and no trace of irony.

Which naturally made it all the harder to deal with. 'I can explain,' Lucy faltered feebly.

'Dinnae bother, hen. I'd strip off for him meself— given the chance!'

Who was the idiot who first told me that women patients were easier to deal with than men? wondered Lucy. She fell back on the old dodge of wearing 'em out and making 'em too breathless to talk. 'Come on now, Trish, you can do better than that. Another good pull and you'll get that heel a good inch nearer your hip than yesterday. . .'

\* \* \*

'Are you quite sure you can manage now?' asked Sally
when they had paid Mike a second and much more
successful visit.

'Positive. Some more quads drill for young Betty
Teviot, another session for Mrs Adams' swollen hand,
and I'm finished for the day.'

'See you tomorrow, then.' And Sally departed for
Physio, while Lucy returned to the women's ward.

Leaving herself some time later, she met Essie, who
was just coming back on duty after an afternoon off. She
waved a newspaper at Lucy. 'Come into the office and
take a look at this,' she invited.

Lucy followed her, frowning. 'I'm not at all sure I
want to ——'

'Oh, yes, you do! You and Mr Lennox have made
"Glasgow Day by Day".'

Dougie's regular column in the *Glasgow Banner*—read
by all the thinking folk in the city! 'That's different.
What does it say?'

'See for yourself.' Essie tossed the paper on to the
desk before stowing her handbag in a drawer.

Lucy pounced. Dougie had headed his contribution
'TO BE OR NOT TO BE A GOOD SAMARITAN?' It
ran as follows.

On Saturday last, two friends out sailing on Loch
Lomond pulled a drowning child from the water
during a sudden squall. Thanks to their skilful and
timely intervention, a boy is alive who otherwise would
surely have died. Not surprisingly, his rescuers themselves were soaked to the skin and, as one of them has
a weekend cottage nearby, sensibly they hurried there
for hot showers and dry clothes.

These are facts. But facts are not enough for the
reporters of the *Sunday Clarion*, who believe that men

and women remove their clothing for one purpose only—even when as exhausted as those two brave rescuers must have been. So in accordance with *Clarion* custom, yesterday, two public-spirited citizens, who deserved nothing but the highest praise, were insulted and smeared.

The lesson is clear, Glaswegians. Do no good deeds. Do not help your fellow men, or you may receive similar attention from the *Sunday Clarion*.

Dougie had not been able to resist going on to take another swipe at the muddy morality of some sections of the press, but Lucy stopped reading at that point. 'Good old Dougie!' she breathed. 'This is marvellous stuff. Do you mind if I take this, Essie?'

'Help yourself, as long as you leave me the crossword.'

'Thanks.' Lucy took out her scissors and cut out the column. 'See you tomorrow, then.'

'And I'll see you before that—on the telly,' Essie called gleefully after her.

In the rush of gratitude she felt towards her cousin, Lucy had almost forgotten that. How would they come across, she and Iain? He had been so serious during that interview. Would that translate as embarrassment? Or guilt? Television could do such funny things to people if they weren't used to it. But surely this column of Dougie's must cheer him up.

Iain wasn't in his consulting-room, so Lucy laid the newspaper cutting on his blotter and scrawled an explanatory note. They met in the doorway just as she was leaving.

'I didn't expect to see you,' he said rather depressingly.

'I came to leave a cutting from the *Banner*, just in case you hadn't seen it. Dougie Fearnan has done us proud.'

'I'm sure that's what he intended to do,' returned Iain, in the same despondent tone, as he came in and shut the door. 'But I'm inclined to think he's probably made things worse.'

Lucy stared. 'However can you think that?'

He stared back at her, his tawny eyes dark and troubled. 'Because those who haven't read the *Clarion* will scuttle all round the city to find a copy. And those who have will be telling themselves that there's never any smoke without fire.'

Lucy hadn't thought of that angle. And given human nature, he probably had a point. But then again, maybe not. 'You're determined to look on the black side, aren't you?' she accused.

'What other side is there?' he asked heavily.

How *dared* he? All right, so he was angry, but it wasn't her fault the boy had fallen in the water, and she'd been libelled too! 'You're impossible!' she stormed. 'Only this morning you told me that we must act as normally as possible, because overreacting and showing embarrassment would make it look as if we really had got something to hide. So I spend all day trying to convince the patients and the staff and the TV people that I was only standing in for a mutual friend by crewing for you on Saturday. While you—you just slouch around behaving exactly as you told me not to!'

Iain's face darkened with displeasure. 'You weren't exaggerating, were you, when you told me you had a nasty temper?' he asked icily. 'At least I haven't tried to lie my way out of the situation.'

'Now, just a minute!' snarled Lucy, sounding and looking remarkably like her mother, only neither of them noticed that. 'I've also been embarrassed and insulted, you know.'

'I'm very sorry that having it known we were out

together on Saturday was such an embarrassment that you had to cook up a cover story.'

'But I thought—and then you said. . .' Lucy waved her hands helplessly. 'You were so different—so withdrawn after that wretched reporter came. And then this morning. . . I thought that *you* were mad at having it known you were out with *me*. I was only trying to—to make things better for you.'

He came and stood over her. The frown was gone. 'Let's get this straight. You thought I was angry because I'd been found out dating you, quite as much as because of the adverse publicity in that rubbishy paper?'

Lucy merely nodded, afraid to speak in case she got it wrong again. 'And that ingenious story of yours was not just your way of telling me goodbye?' he insisted.

This time Lucy shook her head. 'But I did think that was what *you* were telling *me*—both on Saturday night and again this morning.'

He was smiling now. 'For two reasonably articulate people, we've not been communicating too well, have we?'

'That was a helluva thing to happen to two people just getting to—to know each other. I'd go further and say we've failed completely.'

'Fortunately there are other ways of getting on to the same wavelength,' breathed Iain, reaching out and pulling her into his arms. 'So what was I telling you then?' he whispered in her ear after a heady moment or two.

Lucy had never been kissed quite so thrillingly in all her life before, and it took her a moment or two to regain the power of speech. 'That you find me—rather attractive. . .?'

'A considerable understatement. And?'

'Despite the—er—unfortunate happenings the first

time we went out together, you may be willing to try again?'

He chuckled and kissed her again, but briefly. 'Your modesty does you credit—or it might, if I could be sure it's genuine.'

'Call it caution,' said Lucy. 'A girl doesn't assume too much—if she's wise.'

'Careful!' he said, smiling. 'That's the sort of negative thinking that contributed to the misunderstanding.'

'Perhaps—if I were to see enough of you—I might gain some of your confidence.'

'We can but try,' he said. 'So how about starting tomorrow night?'

# CHAPTER SEVEN

'BYE, THEN, Ma. See you tomorrow night.'

'No, see you tonight, Luce.'

'B-but you're off tonight. Won't you be going to the cottage?'

'Got a meeting,' Maggie replied airily. 'I'll not be in for a meal, though—some of us are eating out first.'

'I see.' Lucy paused before asking casually, 'But you're sleeping here?'

'Did I not say so? What's the matter with you, Lucy? You're behaving like an old-fashioned mother!'

'Nothing's the matter, Ma. Only I'm going out myself and—and I wouldn't want either of us to lock the other one out.' Convincing and glib! And I used to be so truthful, she thought.

'First in leaves the hall light on, then—no problem. Have a good time, daughter.' Maggie took two steps towards her car before turning round to ask, 'Did you borrow my *Principles of Joint Surgery*, by any chance? It's not in the bookcase.'

It wasn't? Then it must still be under her bed where I put it along with other incriminating objects in case Iain came in last Saturday, Lucy thought. 'Er—yes,' she said. 'I'll run up and get it for you, shall I?'

'Not to bother—I just like to know where my books are, that's all.' Maggie looked at her watch and swore. 'At this rate, the registrar will be in before me, and I'd not like to give him that satisfaction. ''Bye!'

''Bye, Ma.' Lucy went thoughtfully to her own car. Iain had insisted on picking her up tonight. No problem

119

about that, but as he would also be bringing her home, he would expect to be asked in. And that certainly was *not* on, with Ma either in already or likely to be so any minute. Lucy's imagination got busy with the probable scenario, and she quailed. She had got to be more careful in so many ways. For instance, what would have been Ma's reaction if she'd found that book under her bed? Nothing was worth all this dodging and deceit.

A vivid picture of Iain, tawny eyes alight and teasing, rose to mind, together with the memory of his kisses— and Lucy knew that that particular something definitely was.

The first person she saw at the hospital that morning was Tom Dunning. He watched her park and waited for her to come up with him. 'I saw the news,' he said. 'You were brilliant—both of you.'

'Thanks.' Lucy chewed her bottom lip. 'I wasn't quite straight with you there, was I, Tom?'

'No, you weren't. But your mother's reaction is rather more to the point.'

'Believe it or not, she was tickled to death!'

He nodded. 'Being Maggie, she had to be that—or manic with rage.' He paused. 'Does Iain know yet?' Lucy shook her head. 'So you're choosing your moment,' Tom assumed. 'But you must be the one to tell him, so don't leave it too long—if it matters, that is.'

'It matters,' Lucy admitted quietly as they walked up the steps to Outpatients.

Sister Clyde was in charge today. Amazing how one could sense that, merely by stepping through the door into the main corridor of the unit. 'Good morning, Lucy,' she said, following that with a nicely judged pause. 'You've been having some exciting adventures since we last met.'

'You're putting it more kindly than the *Clarion* did, Sister.'

Sister didn't need to speak; her expression said it all. 'But your cousin went a long way towards redressing the balance in his column yesterday.'

At the sound of footsteps approaching, Lucy put an anxious warning finger to her lips. Sister knew what she was afraid of. 'Mr Murray and Dr Baird are with Mr Lennox in Theatre,' she said. 'Mr Lennox was called in at seven this morning to attend to a badly injured young fireman. While responding to a hoax call, the fire engine was in collision with a car driven by a drunken driver. There's a great deal of wickedness in this world—to balance out such good deeds as yours on Saturday, one supposes. But that's enough of my homespun theology.' Sister switched on to work. 'Mrs Fraser is coming along very nicely now, thanks to her new medication, and a daughter of Mrs Adams' turned up last night and took her mother home to stay with her, so there's one happy ending—not to mention an empty bed. Oh yes—one of the general surgeons is coming to examine Mrs Barr today. And that's about all, I think.'

'Thank you, Sister,' said Lucy.

While conversing, they had been walking slowly down the corridor. Now Sister waved Lucy into the privacy of the office to ask, 'Does Mr Lennox not know whose daughter you are yet, Lucy?'

'No, he doesn't. Not yet.'

'Then I suggest that you tell him quickly, before somebody else does.'

'That's just what Tom Dunning's been telling me.'

'Good.' Sister nodded her approval and Lucy went thoughtfully off to the wards. The advice she was getting was good, and she would act on it. Tonight, perhaps. When Iain took her home. If the evening had gone really well. And if she felt sufficiently sure that his interest in her was strong enough to withstand such a shock! She took a deep breath and entered the men's ward, leaving her private life outside.

Well, not quite. 'Saw you on the telly last night, hen.'

'Fancy that, Mr Craig!'

'It says in the *Banner* that you and Mr Lennox are suing the *Clarion*.'

'That's the first I've heard of it, Mr Buchan,' said Lucy. 'Though I think it would serve them right if we did.'

A chorus of approval and no dissensions. What had happened to Kevin? Lucy turned round to see. He was lying flat, his eyes closed and his face ashen. A vomit bowl waited on his locker. Strange that Sister hadn't mentioned this. 'Oh dear, what's the matter with him?' she asked Mike Craig.

'Hangover,' was the surprising answer.

Lucy stared. 'How in the world. . .?'

'Yesterday was his birthday and some of his pals smuggled in a bottle of whisky. He drank the lot.'

Lucy took another look at the stricken figure. That would be a birthday present he wouldn't forget in a hurry! No wonder Sister hadn't mentioned him; his hangover was a disgrace, not an ailment. The night staff would be getting a rocket for sure. 'Well, at least Kevin's affliction isn't catching,' she said in a louder voice. 'So there's no excuse for the rest of you to slack. Now then!'

By the time the class was over, their new patient was in the ward. How young he looked, sleeping off the anaesthetic. That had been a surgical marathon he had needed. Lucy's turn to help him would come later—this afternoon, perhaps.

Back to the present. 'How did you get on at the Limb

Fitting Centre yesterday afternoon, Mr Buchan?' she asked him.

'It was great, lass. They were very pleased with me—said I must have a good physio.'

'And of course you told them one of the best,' returned Lucy with a smile.

'However did ye guess?'

'It's this gift I have. I think we'll keep your spring weight the same today, but increase the repeats by ten. OK? And when you're ready to change position, give me a shout. I'll only be across the ward with Mr Dewar.'

Mr Dewar, admitted on Saturday after falling from an upstairs window while painting his house, had fractured two spinal vertebrae. Lucy began cautiously as she always did with such patients. 'We'll start at the bottom and work up, Mr Dewar. Can you pull your toes up towards you? No, don't bend your knees.' He tried again, and Lucy asked in a carefully neutral voice if that was all he could manage with his left foot. Always be careful never to alarm the patient.

'Guess so, miss. It feels sort of numb.'

'That happens sometimes.' Lucy put her hands on the tops of his feet. 'Now let's see if I can stop you moving at all.' Dorsiflexors grade three only, even if that. Just a few static back exercises then, to allay any suspicions; then report to Tom.

The shortened treatment only took ten minutes. 'You're letting me off lightly, compared with the other fellows,' considered the patient.

'Only because it's your first day—and we'll be practising again this afternoon.'

Lucy then went in search of Tom, but it was Iain she found in the doctors' room. 'You can't wait until this evening to see me,' he said outrageously.

'I know—isn't it pathetic?' responded Lucy in like

style. 'Actually I'm looking for T—Mr Dunning. A patient of his is showing some neurological deficits I thought I'd better report.'

'He's teaching medical students just now, but if it's really urgent, you'll find Charles in Outpatients.' The consultants only saw each other's patients if one of them was on leave or off duty.

'I'm sure it will do if I catch Mr Dunning after his lecture,' said Lucy.

'Good, because I want to show you the films of Peter Niven, our newest patient.'

They stood close together in front of the viewing screen. Iain's hand was on Lucy's shoulder and she thrilled to the feel. Concentrate on what he's telling you, you idiot! she told herself.

'I don't like doing open reductions on the upper limbs unless it's absolutely necessary,' Iain began, 'and believe me, in this case, it was. I just couldn't take any chances with the radial nerve, so I had to plate the humerus. The fracture was compound and there was considerable loss of muscle tissue from triceps.'

He changed the X-rays and Lucy saw that the left tibia was a mess. 'Oh, God!' she breathed.

'Exactly. But wait until you see his right leg.'

'Surely it can't be worse that that?'

'Unfortunately it is—multiple fractures and extensive soft tissue damage as well. We managed to fix up a collateral circulation, but it'll be a miracle if we don't have to amputate.'

'Oh, no!' Lucy gasped.

'I know just how you feel. A fine young man, a top amateur athlete with an important job, is likely to be crippled for life because one mindless moron called the fire brigade for a joke, while another drove drunkenly round the streets.' Iain's voice was full of sad disgust.

'What about the drunken driver?' she asked.

'He got off scot free because the driver of the fire engine was, by contrast, a damn good driver who managed to avoid a head-on collision and bounced off a brick wall instead. There's no justice.'

'It would be very interesting to see how the *Sunday Clarion* would report that,' said Lucy through compressed lips.

'They wouldn't—no scope for porn,' Iain retorted crisply. A slight increase of pressure on her shoulder and he let her go, turning round to lean against the wall and look down at her in a way that Lucy was finding very exciting. 'You came across quite splendidly on the box last night,' he said.

'So did you. All stiff upper lip and great nobility.'

That evoked a broad smile. 'My sister thought I appeared distinctly surly.'

Perhaps that sister wasn't just a convenient invention after all! 'I prefer my reading,' said Lucy with a provocative little smile.

'So do I.' The look in his eyes was a caress. 'I really appreciated your agreeing to visit the boy so willingly. Was it much of an ordeal?'

'None at all. They had everything ready when I got there, and then they told me exactly what to say and do. All very proper. The whole thing was over in less than fifteen minutes.' Lucy paused. 'Afterwards, the producer asked me to go for a drink, but I didn't.'

'Quite right. The very idea!'

'I don't think he had any nefarious designs on me.'

'If he hadn't, then he must be either crazy or past it.'

'Thanks for the warning. I can see I shall have to keep a careful watch on you!'

Iain opened his mouth to cap that, just as the tap-tapping of Lois's high heels sounded outside in the corridor. By tacit agreement, they drew apart, and Lucy muttered that she'd better be going.

As the two girls passed one another, the look of loathing that Lois threw her way gave Lucy a considerable jolt. But again, as once before, she asked herself, what harm can she possibly do to me?

Reporting to Tom about Mr Dewar's muscle weakness and loss of sensation. Being congratulated on her powers of observation. Buckling on Mike Craig's cast brace and taking him for a walk. And finally, before lunch, a round of the elderly men with hip fractures. Only a few of them, unlike the many on the other side of the corridor. What a pity I can't get both sexes together for their exercises, thought Lucy. It might liven them up. But for that, she would need a day-room or a small gym, and these refinements had been in the pipeline for so long that nobody really expected them to materialise. Glasgow General Hospital had been built in the last century, when patients were kept in bed until the day they were discharged—and physiotherapists hadn't been invented.

After last night's TV exposure, going to the canteen would inevitably mean whispers and sidelong glances, so Lucy settled for an apple and a bar of chocolate in Physio, while she wrote up her morning's treatment notes. Back on the unit, she told Sally she still had things to do in the men's ward and would join her later.

Another brief treatment for Mr Dewar, and not a word about his symptoms. Bad news was for doctors to give—one of the reasons that Lucy had shrunk from following in the family footsteps.

Mike Craig was quite good on his crutches now and wanted to know why she wouldn't let him keep them by him. 'Not until you can put that brace on and off without help.'

'That's no' fair!'

'Fairer than having you hopping about without it, as you'd be tempted to do. And then perhaps cracking the new bone that's forming.'

'Ye're a hard wumman, Lucy Trent,' he sighed.

'That's why I got the job. How's Kevin this afternoon?'

A groan from the next bed was answer enough. But no cheek from him yet. 'That's some hangover he's got there,' observed Lucy.

'Out of practice, I reckon,' Mike said with a grin.

When Iain, Charles, Lois and Sister Clyde came in to see the young fireman, Lucy crossed the ward and stood quietly by, waiting for the latest bulletin.

'His BP's still on the low side,' muttered Iain, frowning at the chart.

'He's had four pints of whole blood,' was Lois's contribution.

'Three, Doctor,' corrected Sister. 'He still has one to come.' Lois scowled.

'Is he complaining of much pain, Sister?'

'No, sir, but he's just being brave—I can always tell.' She handed Iain the drugs chart before he could ask for it.

He gave her a brief smile of approval for her understanding before writing rapidly. 'There, that should do the trick without rendering him too sleepy.' Iain looked round. 'I thought I saw—oh, you're here, Lucy.' Another fleeting smile, but for her, warm and intimate this time. 'Usual routine: active movement wherever possible and plenty of deep breathing exercises. A chest infection is unlikely, but it's something he can do without.'

'Do you wish me to start treating today, sir?'

A quick twitch of his humorous mobile mouth at the

formality. 'Just the breathing exercises—the rest will keep until tomorrow.'

'Thank you—as I thought, sir.'

At that, a sneer appeared on Lois's face, as much as to say how easy it was to be wise after the event. She really was very jealous. Was she actually in love with Iain, or was it only her pride that was hurt? Just as well for all concerned that she would be moving to another hospital at the end of the month. Lucy wondered where she was going.

As they all left the ward, Sister offered tea to the little group, but Lucy declined when Lois accepted. Besides, she hadn't been given Sally's help so as to have time for mid-afternoon tea parties!

Trisha was miserable. The skin on her injured leg was red, swollen and sore. 'It's the bluidy brace,' she said gloomily.

'It shouldn't be—it's made of stainless steel. More likely, it's an allergic reaction to whatever antiseptic they're swabbing you with. I'll have a word with Sister.'

'Thanks. I telt Barbie Doll about it this morning, but damn all's happened so far.'

Poor Lois—what a name they'd given her! Best to pretend she hadn't heard that. So Lucy just said, 'Sister will know what to do.' But they would still all be there, drinking tea in the office, including Lois. Ask Sally to pop her head round the door, then. Brilliant! If Lois got a rocket for forgetting, Lucy wanted no part of it. Lois disliked her quite enough already.

As Sally sped away, Lucy coaxed, 'Come on, now. Let's do some strengthening exercises for your good leg. I know how much you hate that, so it'll take your mind off that itching.'

'Takin' me across to see Kev'd work better.'

'Stick first and carrot later,' returned Lucy firmly.

'You come o' fightin' stock, I'm thinking,' grumbled Trisha. How right she was, if only she'd known it!

No dramatic changes among the old ladies, all inching their way slowly back to their former physical fitness— or frailty, according to how you looked at it. No time to spare, and yet the afternoon was dragging. Just because I'm looking forward so much to the evening, Lucy admitted to herself.

At last there was only Peter Niven to be treated. He had been lying with his eyes closed, but he opened them as Lucy approached. 'Temperature, or yet another jab?' he asked with a gallant attempt at humour.

Lucy felt a lump forming in her throat. Bravery like this always made her feel very humble. 'I only want you to do some breathing exercises—they won't be painful,' she added, but she changed her mind when she saw the heavy bruising on his body. Carefully she supported his lower ribs with her hands. 'Try to feel that you're pushing against my hands. Gently now.'

But Peter Niven was not the man for half measures. Lucy realised that his basal expansion must be at least five inches! She remembered that Iain had told her that their new patient was an athlete. 'That was fantastic, Mr Niven,' she congratulated him. 'An opera singer wouldn't have a better pair of lungs.'

He gave her a wavering smile. 'Maybe Scottish Opera will take me on, then—if I have to leave the Fire Service.'

'From your speaking voice, I'd say you'd be in with a jolly good chance,' said Lucy. 'Have you done any singing?'

'Only Country and Western.' A spasm of pain crossed his face and he shifted slightly.

'What is it?' she asked.

'My right leg—cramp.'

Carefully Lucy readjusted the pillows supporting it. 'Better?' she queried.

'Much—it's going away now.'

But there would be many more such spasms. And nothing Lucy could do to help. There was nobody in the office when she went off duty, so she left a note for Sister. Peter Niven was too much of a stoic to complain of his own accord.

The first thing that Lucy did on reaching home was to stick a card over Maggie's nameplate again—Blu-tak *and* Sellotape. Because if it fell off when Iain rang the doorbell, the evening would be over before it began. They were going to a concert and wouldn't be eating until afterwards, so Lucy made a sandwich to eat while running a bath. Lunch had been almost a non-event, and a rumbling tum during the quiet passages would hardly enhance her iamge. And then came the big problem of deciding what to wear. In the end, she settled for a neat-waisted, full-skirted dress of Indian cotton in muted blues and greens which did wonders for her figure.

Iain was prompt to the minute, and the doorbell shrilled as Lucy was tidying away her make-up. When she opened the door, his tawny eyes swept over her with open approval. He wasn't looking so bad himself in a pale lightweight suit, crisp cream shirt and some club tie or other. Correction. He was looking terrific—bronzed, healthy and vital—*and* he probably knew it. Lucy decided it was time they stopped admiring each other, so she said, 'Hello.'

For answer, he bent and kissed her lingeringly on the mouth. 'Nothing like starting the way you mean to go on,' he said provocatively. 'You look absolutely fantastic, by the way.'

'How kind of you to notice!' A demure downward glance, to show off her long lashes.

'Did you think I wouldn't?'

Of course not, or she wouldn't have gone to all that trouble! But she said that silently. 'Can I offer you a drink—or isn't there time?'

Iain looked at his watch, while Lucy looked at his hand, firm and strong with a faint dusting of fine gold hairs. 'There's time,' he decided. 'And if you have such a thing, a dry sherry would be most acceptable.'

'I think I can find some,' she said lightly, shutting the door and leading the way to the living-room, with its wide balconied window and the view of distant Ben Lomond. She fetched savoury biscuits from the kitchen and poured two sherries.

Iain had been looking round the room, and as she handed him his drink he said, 'You've fairly fallen on your feet here, Lucy. How did you find this place?'

'It belongs to a—relative—and most of the time I have it to myself. Do have some biscuits,' she added nervously. His curiosity was natural, but not bargained for, though it should have been. And every evasive reply was piling up the deceit.

'Travels about a lot, then, does he—or are we talking about a she?'

'Who?'

'Your generous relative.'

'Not really.'

'Generous?'

'I meant the travelling bit. She works in Glasgow, but lives mainly in the country.' A bolstering swig of sherry. 'And where do you live, Iain?'

'On the south side—in Pollokshields.'

'Nice and near the hospital, then.'

He grinned crookedly, showing excellent teeth. 'Too

near, sometimes! I often tell Charles and Jim that they'd not be so keen to call me in if I lived out in the sticks like Tom. He and his wife have a lovely house near Busby.'

Lucy just managed not to tell him that she knew that. And if she'd also told him why—that the Dunnings and her parents had all been students together—then the fat really would have been in the fire! 'That's a very attractive part of the world, I'm told,' she said brightly. 'Let me top up your glass.'

'No, thanks—and that's no reflection on your sherry, which is excellent. You do yourself well, Lucy.'

If only she could have told him the truth: that it was a present to her mother from a grateful patient. But this wasn't the time to break the news. That was for later, after a happy evening, over coffee perhaps—except that she couldn't risk that. Not with Maggie liable to breeze in at any moment.

Lucy sighed, and Iain frowned at her in mock disapproval. 'I'm sorry that the prospect of an evening in my company should fill you with such sadness.'

She pulled herself together. 'There are sighs and sighs,' she said. 'And that was definitely not a sorrowful one.'

'What a relief!' he responded gravely. 'Now, are you going to wear this beautiful jacket, or will I carry it for you?'

'Oh Iain, how kind,' she smiled.

'I am—and thoughtful too.'

'It was one of the first things I noticed about you,' she claimed laughingly, as she pulled the outer door shut behind them. This was better. Light-hearted banter she could cope with—and match.

They kept it up all the way to the concert hall, and Lucy said as they mounted the steps, 'I'm really looking forward to this. This is the concert out of all the series that I particularly wanted to hear, only it was sold out long ago—or so they told me. However did you get tickets at such short notice?'

'I didn't,' said Iain. I got the whole series months back when booking opened.'

'Ah, so I'm standing in for your regular concert-going chum, am I?'

A knowing look told her what he thought of that for an unsubtle bit of fishing. 'I'll tell you this much,' he allowed. 'Play your cards right and you'll get to all the others as well.'

'That is some bribe,' she considered. 'And I'd probably take it—if only I knew what playing my cards right entailed.'

He took her arm and tucked it under his. 'Go on the way you're doing and you're more than halfway there.'

'Lovely!' But halfway to what? Lucy wondered as they took their seats just as the lights began to dim. Was she still on trial for the post of temporary girlfriend—or did his interest go deeper? Knowing the answer to that would be a great help when planning the great revelation.

A rousing Elgar overture and Beethoven's Sixth Symphony inevitably evoked tumultuous applause at the end of the first half. It was hot in the auditorium, and Lucy readily agreed when Iain suggested a long cool drink in the foyer.

She regretted that the minute they stepped outside. 'Little Lucy Trent, by all that's marvellous!' she heard in a voice that was vaguely familiar. She spun round to come face to face with the young doctor who had taken over Jock's practice.

'Er—hello,' she mumbled.

When he had finished pumping her hand up and down, Robert Gordon introduced his wife, obliging Lucy

to introduce Iain. 'Lennox, Lennox,' he repeated.
'That's a name that rings a bell.' He didn't pursue that,
though, saying instead, 'Tell me, Lucy, how's old Jock
these days? He hasn't been to a BMA meeting for some
time now.'

'No, he's not getting out much lately. His arthritis has
been very troublesome.' Nearly as troublesome as this
meeting is to me! she thought. Don't, *please* don't ask
about Ma——

'And how's that ball of fire you call mother?' Robert
asked next, his telepathy obviously out of order.

'Fine, thank you—very busy.' Safe enough, when that
described almost all mothers.

'I believe you. Good old Ma——'

Lucy didn't so much drop her smart green bag as hurl
it to the floor, where it obligingly burst open and
scattered its contents. By the time they had all four gone
down on hands and knees to rake around among all the
feet and retrieve her bits and pieces, the final warning
bell was sounding.

Upright again, Robert said, 'Look here, how about
meeting afterwards for a drink?'

'I don't know. . .' Lucy looked helplessly at Iain.

'That would have been nice,' he said firmly, 'but we
have a table booked for supper, so I'm afraid there'll be
no time.'

'Ah well, can't be helped. But give my regards to Jock
and Ma——'

'I will, Robert, I will. They'll be so interested to hear
we met. 'Bye now,' said Lucy hastily.

'Correct me if I'm wrong,' said Iain, unsettling her
just when she'd begun to feel safe. 'Your maternal
grandfather is a retired GP known to his intimates as
Jock. Right?'

'Well done,' said Lucy, subsiding thankfully into her seat.

'Not at all. The clues were all there. And your mother?'

She caught her breath and coughed, before asking warily, 'Well? What about her?'

'Do you have to sound so truculent? After all, his description was rather intriguing. How many middle-aged female balls of fire do you know?'

'Several. But I'd sooner describe my mother as—as energetic.'

'He was exaggerating, then, was he?'

'I would say so.'

'What a relief,' said Iain drolly, as the conductor returned to the platform. 'Female balls of fire are not my favourite people,' he confided needlessly in Lucy's ear a split second before the music started.

An hour or so of Mozart at his most melodic and romantic quite chased away all thoughts of fireballs, female or otherwise, and they were both in a state of elation as they walked to the car. 'That was sheer bliss!' breathed Lucy.

'I suspect that a real music-lover would call that a right pot-boiler of a programme,' Iain returned ruefully.

'A musical snob might, but as far as I'm concerned that was exactly the sort of programme I like best.'

'You're sounding truculent again,' he teased. 'And there's absolutely no need. It was exactly what I prefer too. What a lot we have in common.'

'Yes,' she agreed, knowing that was true—but also wondering if it would be enough when he knew the worst.

'Here we are.' Iain unlocked the car. 'So in you get, and let's go and find out if we have the same taste in food. Hungry?'

'Famished!'

'I do like a girl who likes her food. My last girlfriend but one was perpetually on a diet. It was very boring.'

'Was that why she got the chop?'

'You could have put that more gracefully,' he considered. 'However, the answer is no—not entirely.'

'I knew I was right. You *are* very hard to please.'

'Just as with music, I know how I like my women.'

'You make us sound like—like some sort of saleable commodity,' Lucy said reprovingly.

'That's not a bad analogy,' he returned, unabashed. 'Considering the high price some women put on themselves.'

'Just as nearly all men do—and rarely with as much justification,' Lucy retaliated.

More for effect than from anger, Iain beat his fist on the steering wheel. 'Dammit, I knew she was a feminist!'

'Nonsense! Though I do agree with them that it's a man's world. Only I realise that it always will be, and since we can't change that, we'd better make the best of it. But half the male sex being awful doesn't stop me liking the other half. And quite a lot—in a few cases.'

'Are you trying to tell me something?' he wondered as he parked the car at the pavement's edge outside a small restaurant with attractive fringed canopies above its windows.

'Just this. If you play your cards right,' Lucy was quoting his words back at him deliberately, 'then *you* could be in with a chance.'

He stared at her in disbelief, and Lucy stared as steadily back, realising that this was probably the first time that any girl had challenged Iain Lennox on his own terms. And she wouldn't be doing so either, if she'd had the least hope that this thing had more than the briefest of shelf-lives. No, this was definitely not the way she had envisaged the evening going!

And then, to her admiration, he began to laugh. Small quiet chuckles at first, then deeper and louder, with the shaking of his shoulders keeping pace. 'Lucy Trent,' he said at last, 'you are without doubt the most surprising and refreshing girl I ever knew!'

'What a coincidence! That's almost exactly what that TV producer said,' she returned provocatively.

'And you had the nerve to tell me he didn't have any designs on you!'

'A girl doesn't like to boast,' she murmured, blue eyes wide and guileless.

Iain's answering look was a heady mixture of admiration and challenge. 'Only time will tell just where it is we're going,' he said softly, 'but one thing is clear—the journey will be anything but dull!'

The restaurant was Italian; small unpretentious and authentic. Its back windows were almost at the river's edge and the view across the Clyde was one of pleasant, modern housing in a tree-dotted landscape. A mute comment on Glasgow's shifting fortunes; once, there had been docks and cranes over there.

Iain followed Lucy's glance. 'That was the Garden Festival site,' he told her.

'I thought it must have been.' Lucy knew it, having gone there several times with Maggie that summer. Yet she dared not admit it—not yet. The need for such deceit was fast becoming a sorrow and a shame. Angrily she put away her feelings of guilt. 'You're very clever at finding lovely places to eat,' she said, smiling brilliantly across the table.

'I've had a lot of practice,' Iain returned wryly.

'Well, you would have, wouldn't you?' she asked.

'Not many bachelors I've known could be bothered to cook for themselves.'

Iain cupped his chin in his hands, placed his elbows on the table and stared into her eyes. 'And what about spinsters?' he queried.

'I can't answer for them all, but this one likes cooking.'

'Likes cooking,' he echoed. 'That's another entry on the credit side. If you go on like this, I shall have to start a new page!'

'And if you go on like that, I shall have to buy a bigger hat,' Lucy was answering as the waiter returned to take their order.

The food was as good as Lucy's first impression of the place had promised. Better still was the mood in which the meal was eaten. No more scoring of points, no more references to past experiences; just open and honest enjoyment of the present as they explored each other's interests and points of view. Their delight in each other grew with each new proof of basic accord. And through it all was woven the bright and thrilling thread of a strong mutual attraction; the first thing that had brought them together, and potentially the most rewarding thing of all.

'Time to go,' said Iain, when all that could be seen outside were thousands of reflected lights dancing in the darkness of the river. 'Unless you want another coffee,' he added indulgently. Lucy had already had three.

She smiled and shook her head. 'No, thank you. It's— all been quite perfect.' And she wasn't just referring to the food.

'Yes, hasn't it?' he asked quietly, and she knew he had understood. 'But the evening's not over yet.'

How was she going to tell him that she couldn't ask him up to the flat? Lucy put it off until Iain drove into the car park of the Court. 'Rather different from Saturday's homecoming, isn't it?' he asked eagerly.

'Totally. We're not at cross-purposes tonight. At least . . .'

'You're getting ready to slam the door in my face,' he said, though it was obviously the last thing he expected.

'Iain, I'm dreadfully sorry, but my flatmate will be there! She wasn't expected to be, but she suddenly decided to stay tonight—and there wasn't a thing I could do about it.'

'Of course not—as it's her flat,' he returned reasonably. He had parked near the entrance. Now he reversed the car into a dark corner under some overhanging trees.

When he took her in his arms, Lucy went eagerly, clinging to him and returning kiss for kiss. She strained nearer, the gear-lever digging into her leg, but she hardly noticed.

And then they were illuminated by powerful headlights sweeping over them. They broke apart. The car was parked, and in the instant before the lights were extinguished, Lucy read her mother's number-plate. Quite the most powerful turn-off possible in the circumstances!

But now it was dark again. Once more Iain pulled her close, and Lucy wound her arm around his neck as she surrendered to his eager, demanding mouth. Except that this time, for her, the spell was broken. Reality had intruded.

When a second car swept past them with the same revealing results, Iain attributed her apparent loss of enthusiasm to that. 'You'd better come round to my place tomorrow night,' he whispered. 'I'm on call, but given luck, I'll not be needed—and at least there'll be no searchlights!'

'I'm so sorry,' Lucy whispered miserably.

'Me too, sweetheart.' When a third car went by, he asked despairingly, 'Why couldn't you have found a flat where the neighbours stay home at nights?'

'I'll start looking for one tomorrow.'

He pulled her close once more and kissed her, but briefly. 'Lucy, you're so sweet.'

'Don't you mean irritating?'

'Certainly not! I'm quite sure you didn't arrange that procession.' Another kiss, before he sighed and said, 'Come on, I'll walk you to the door.'

Then in the porch he said, 'This is for all the neighbours who missed the previous performances.' Then he folded her close and kissed her with a depth and passion fit to melt her very bones. 'Tomorrow night we'll pick up where we had to leave off tonight,' he breathed huskily when he let her go.

It was some time before Lucy trusted her legs to carry her up the three flights of stairs to the flat.

# CHAPTER EIGHT

'YOU weren't long after me last night, Luce.'

Lucy buried her nose in her teacup and agreed, 'No, Ma,' in a muffled voice.

'Nice evening?'

'Terrific, thanks. How was your meeting?'

'Very boring. More toast?'

'No thanks—must dash.' Lucy leapt up from the breakfast table.

'You're a real chip off the old block,' Maggie called after her affectionately.

On her way out Lucy called, 'I'll be out again tonight, Ma.'

'That's all right, Luce—so shall I.'

No questions. Maggie was not that sort of mother. Which made it easier to go on going out with her least favourite person behind her back. Lucy wrinkled her nose. I wish I hadn't thought that thought in those words, she mused. It sort of puts me in the wrong, and I don't think I am. Not really. . . Even heavier morning traffic than usual obliged her to shelve her muddled thoughts and concentrate on her driving. And when she did arrive at the hospital, she slid into her professional persona along with a clean tunic and trousers.

It turned out to be one of those days when nothing went right. Two nurses short meant that Sister wasn't in her office to provide the usual update, and thumbing through the Kardex instead was a poor substitute for Sister's concise comments. Naturally, the girls were behind in the wards, which meant Lucy's timetable was up the spout. A morning of treating haphazardly here and there, and only a shortened class squeezed in just before lunch.

'You'll be lucky, I'm afraid,' sighed Lucy when Mr Watson said he hoped she'd be coming to put him through his paces again later on.

But the morning was a picnic, compared with the afternoon, because Mrs Cumnock kept Sally in the department, to cover for another physio who had gone to have a tooth out. 'It must be a very large tooth if it's going to take all the afternoon,' growled Lucy when apprised of this.

'My feelings exactly,' returned Sally,' but you know what she's like.'

'I'm beginning to,' Lucy returned grimly. Out of sight, out of mind, seemed to be their superintendent's attitude to the wards. 'Bloody woman's an ostrich,' she muttered, stumping out of the office after taking Sally's call—and cannoning into Iain, coming in.

He steadied her with a much more comprehensive grip than the collision actually required, which did a lot to cool her anger, while simultaneously increasing her pulse rate. 'Who's an ostrich?' he asked with a grin.

'My unrevered lady boss.'

'She looks more like a hippo to me, but I get your drift.' Having reduced Lucy to giggles, Iain let her go. 'What's she done this time?'

'Only kept Sally on Outpatients today. One girl is off.'

Iain frowned into space. 'There's a half a dozen of them down there. Surely they could have shared out the work between them? And there's something else. Tom was saying the other day that an extra full-time physio was appointed especially for Ortho when this department was expanded a couple of years back. Perhaps it's time we reminded Madam Cumnock of that.' His frown disappeared as he looked down at Lucy again. 'All set for tonight?'

'You must be joking!' she groaned. 'If I get away from here by seven it'll be a miracle. I haven't finished my morning's work yet.'

Iain frowned once more. 'Concentrate on your most serious cases, then. Now I'm going straight down to have a word with Mrs Cumnock. It's time she got her act together. This isn't the only unit that's not adequately covered.'

'Thanks, Iain—I think you're wonderful,' said Lucy as, with one final bright glance, he strode away to carry out his threat. Except for the inevitable summer holidays, they were fully staffed at present. Lucy suspected that Mrs Cumnock wouldn't be enjoying the next few minutes.

Despite adhering to Iain's orders to concentrate on the most serious cases, it was well after six by the time Lucy returned to Physio to get out of uniform.

Free at last of daytime restraints, she allowed her thoughts to dwell wholly on Iain as she stepped into the shower. What a surprise—and a contradiction—he had turned out to be! If other people's opinions were to be taken as fact, then he was a chauvinist and a womaniser. Lucy had soon stopped believing all of that, and since last night had discarded that picture altogether. Such a man would have been sulky and bad-tempered in the face of those doorstep frustrations—not understanding and even wryly amused as Iain had been. There was a much nicer side to his nature that Maggie, for one, was quite unaware of. Lucy looked forward to opening her mother's eyes. But she felt less hopeful about the reverse process of showing Iain the real Maggie. But she would manage it somehow—given that their mutual attraction and liking really were as strong as she believed.

Showered and dried, Lucy put on clean underwear, a boldly printed cotton skirt and toning cherry blouse with scoop neckline and full puff sleeves. She looked fresh, young and—she hoped—also rather alluring. Because tonight was very special. She could feel it.

In the car park, she saw Lois getting out of her car. After an afternoon of freedom, Lois was now presumably returning to duty. Lucy might have felt sorry for her on that score, but for Lois's strange look of mingled triumph and dislike as she passed without answering Lucy's brief greeting. See if I care, thought Lucy. I bet I know which one of us is going to have the nicest evening!

Iain's flat was only minutes from the hospital—on the top floor of a spacious detached Victorian mansion in a broad, tree-lined avenue of similar houses, now too big to be maintained by one family. Most of them had been converted into flats. Lucy pressed the appropriate button on the panel and said, 'It's me—Lucy,' into the speaker when Iain answered the buzz.

The massive front door was released with a click as he purred, 'Come on up, darling,' setting her sensory nerves a-tingle. Never before had she been so sensitive to a man—indeed, she had often thought her friends were exaggerating their own reactions. No longer; because there really was something in all that stuff about Mr Right!

He stood in the doorway, watching her ascend the last short flight of stairs. 'You look good enough to eat,' he said slowly, his tawny eyes sweeping over her.

'Don't scare me,' she said jerkily—and it wasn't the climb that had made her breathless. 'I've come to be fed, not served up on a plate!'

'And fed you shall be—all in good time. But first. . .'

He drew her inside and shut the door with a decisive thud.

His kiss was lengthy, satisfying and sweet, and afterwards he murmured against her cheek, 'I've been longing to do that all day. Have you any idea how enticing you look in that absurd uniform?'

Lucy chuckled softly in her throat. 'If I had, I'd have kept it on and not bothered to change!'

Iain laughed too, then held her at arm's length for another appraisal. 'I'm glad you did. That outfit is even better,' he decided. Another embrace, another of those heady kisses, and then he took her hand and led her into a huge and sunny living-room, which had dormer windows to the south and west, acres of white paint, rows and rows of books, numerous roomy armchairs and a very inviting-looking sofa. On a low table in front of this, a tray with glass tumblers and a large jug of something fruity stood ready. 'My summertime answer to the aperitif question,' Iain explained as he poured out.

Lucy savoured her drink. 'Mmm, lovely! This isn't just another variation on the Pimms' theme, is it?'

He twisted his handsome face into a most ferocious scowl. 'How can you suspect me of anything so banal?' he wondered. 'There's vintage champagne in this, my girl.'

'I *knew* he had designs on me,' she sighed theatrically.

'You—and the whole orthopaedic department knows it too, I imagine. You don't need to be clairvoyant to know that.'

But being clairvoyant could be a whole heap of help in deciding the exact nature of his designs. Lucy felt pretty sure by now that she'd be going along with whatever it was he had in mind, but even in these emancipated days a girl couldn't help having the occasional dream about white lace, orange blossom and permanency.

Iain served up a delicious meal of iced cherry soup, chicken salad and crisp new rolls, with melon and strawberries for dessert. 'I thought you said you didn't like cooking,' said Lucy when they exchanged their seats at the round dining-table for that inviting sofa at the other end of the room.

'I don't,' he confirmed, 'but fortunately there's a brace of energetic sisters in the next road who do. And they put up these rather superior take-aways.'

'Superior is the word,' agreed Lucy, as she accepted a coffee. 'We could do with something like this on my side of the city.'

'You told me you liked cooking.'

'I do, but unfortunately I don't always have the time.'

'I'm disappointed,' he said, sitting down beside her close enough for their shoulders to touch.

'Don't be,' she responded. 'I do get around to it—sometimes.'

'Like when?'

'Like—some time you happen to be both off duty and rather hungry?'

'Tomorrow, then,' he returned with evident satisfaction. 'More coffee?'

'No, thanks,' said Lucy.

'In that case. . .' He took her cup from her and put it on the table with his own. 'Some unfinished business from yesterday. . .' he breathed as he took her in his arms.

To Lucy, it felt absolutely right to be there, responding to kisses that weren't just eager, but tender as well; plumbing depths of emotion way beyond the merely physical. If Iain was feeling as she was, then surely——

Came the shrilling of the telephone and muttered imprecations from Iain as he released Lucy with reluctance and got up to answer it. He returned looking dejected. 'Darling, I'm sorry——'

'But that was the hospital, and they need you.'

'You've got it.' He came swiftly across the room and hauled her to her feet. They stood face to face, bodies touching, their hands clasped together at their sides. 'Do you think you could always be this understanding?' Iain asked softly.

'I could try,' she whispered back.

'I've no idea how long I'll be. . .'

'But however long it is, I'll still be here when you get back.'

'You couldn't guess how good that sounds,' murmured Iain. One last kiss, and he was gone.

Lucy stood on the landing, listening to his receding footsteps. When she heard the outside door clang shut, she went back into the flat and started on the washing up. Only after she had dried the last cup and was opening doors to find out where to put things, did she discover the dishwasher. I might have guessed, she mused with a tender little half-smile. Trust Iain to have every aid to comfort and efficiency! He would run his personal and domestic life with the energy and expertise he brought to his work. A man to lean on and look up to: What more could a girl ask for?

He had asked her if she could always be so understanding—which might have been a significant question. Lucy decided she thought it was. She went back into the living-room, picked up that day's *Glasgow Banner* and sat down, trying to read, while she waited impatiently to find out.

It was after ten when Iain returned. His step was heavy, his look sombre and brooding. Lucy had jumped up and run towards him as he entered the room, but she stopped several paces from him, unaccountably anxious. He was tense, and the tension was all around him like an impenetrable wall. 'Could—shall I make you some coffee?' Lucy asked uncertainly.

'What I need is a good strong drink,' he muttered savagely, striding past her and across the room to a tall mahogany cupboard, where he poured himself a formidable treble whisky.

Lucy had never seen him so deeply disturbed—not even when those reporters had come to the cabin. That emergency must have been something quite exceptional! She crept nearer, colliding with a chair as she went.

Iain swung round at the sound and regarded her stonily. Lucy stared worriedly back. Not a trace remained of the blissful accord they had shared before he was called out. 'Was it—very awful, then?' she asked timidly.

'You could say that.' His tone was harsh and clipped.

'Somebody you know—somebody close to you?' Yes, that was the reason. What else could account for so black a mood? 'Oh, my dear——'

'There were two in the car—both strangers to me,' he said baldly, having known at once what she was getting at. 'The driver was able to go home after treatment, but the passenger—an elderly man—had to be admitted with multiple rib fractures which will no doubt lead to a chest infection, requiring your devoted attention over the next few days.'

That recital, delivered in such biting tones, had stopped Lucy in her tracks. 'Is that—all?' she asked, bewildered. Apart from anything else, that would have been well within the competence of the registrar, so why had Iain been called in at all?

'Were you in his shoes, you'd probably consider it enough,' he retorted.

'I meant—I mean. . .Oh, surely you know what I

mean! Iain, what's wrong? What's happened? Everything was—so wonderful before you went out.'

He finished his drink, made to pour another, suddenly realised what he was doing and shut the cupboard with a gesture of disgust. Then he swung round to face Lucy again. 'I dare say it was—from your point of view! Everything was going exactly according to plan, wasn't it?'

'I—I don't know what you mean,' she quavered, though beginning to be terribly afraid that she did.

'Oh, I think you do,' he challenged icily.

Tawny eyes and smoky blue ones locked together in a long silent stare. 'You've f-found out, haven't you?' Lucy asked at last on a whisper, miserably aware, even as she spoke, that putting it that way was tantamount to admitting to calculated deceit. 'What I mean is—you know about—my mother. I was going to tell you——'

'Of course you were,' he said with open contempt. 'What a pity somebody else got in first!'

'Surely you can see why I didn't?'

'I *know* why you didn't—but I'd be—interested to hear your version.'

'It was only because you don't like Maggie—my mother.'

'That is mutual,' he reminded her.

'But it's worse on your side.' He looked sceptical at that. Why didn't he let fly? Lash her with harsh words she could repudiate? That would clear the air. This deliberate holding back was impossible to cope with. 'If I'd told you right at the beginning, we'd never have had the chance to—to get close, would we? Because I'd not even have got my job.'

Another contemptuous look. 'I hope I'd have been sufficiently professional to recognise that you were far and away the best candidate. As to the closeness——' he had spat out that word as if it sullied his tongue '—if you'd told me, at least we'd have got to know one another honestly and openly, without deceit. But that wouldn't have suited Maggie's book, would it?'

'Now I *really* do not know what you mean!'

'Come off it, Lucy—I know that you and your mother deliberately planned to make a fool of me!'

'How dare you! We never did any such thing!' Lucy denied hotly. 'What an appalling idea!'

'I couldn't agree more with you there—but I've been told all about the plot.'

'Then you've been told a pack of lies! There was no plot to—to make a fool of you, as you put it. It just seemed—well, politic in the circumstances, to see if I could land the job on my own merits. And then to——'

'I've already told you that I'd have judged you on your merits alone.'

'That's very easy to say—now!' Lucy snapped.

'Are you suggesting I wouldn't have done so?' he demanded harshly.

'Well, you're not being exactly objective now, are you?'

'What the hell would you expect?' he thundered. 'You deceive me, lead me on——'

'Now just you wait a minute!' Maggie's fiery genes were definitely uppermost now. 'It didn't take you long to make a pass at me—and a pretty chauvinistic way you went about it too! I hadn't expected that. All right, so I didn't discourage you—I'll admit that. I liked you, you see! Though now I'm damned if I can see why!'

'And you'd better believe that goes for me too!' he roared.

They glared at one another with unabated fury for a long five seconds until Lucy said scathingly, 'In that case, your informant has done us both a service—no

matter how slanderous and inaccurate her account!'.
Because of course it was a female who had told him, and
Lucy would have laid bets that she knew which one. She
stalked out of the room, snatched up her bag from the
hall table and banged out of the flat with a crash that
even Maggie at her most furious couldn't have exceeded.

That was a pretty good exit line, she thought as she
clattered down the stairs. He wouldn't have expected
that! Had probably expected her to grovel and plead.
Yes, Lucy girl, you certainly scored a bull's eye there!
she told herself. She flounced out of the house with a
second slam and got into her car, literally trembling with
rage.

Her anger buoyed her up all the way home. Iain was
arrogant, he was hateful, he was everything Maggie had
said he was—and more! He was a shallow, vain, conceited woman-chaser, who had only been so angry
because he thought he'd been made a fool of. Yes, *that*
was what he was!

Still in the grip of fury when she reached home, Lucy
crashed her car into the low wall bounding the parking
bay and bent the bumper. Another black mark against
Iain—it was his fault!

Almost weeping with rage, Lucy steamed up the stairs
to the flat, where she hurled herself into a chair. She
looked round the room. Was it really only yesterday that
she and Iain had drunk sherry and laughed together in
this room at the start of that perfect evening? The only
flaw had been that unexpected meeting with the
Gordons.

Lucy found herself going over it all again. She should
have told Iain last night—better still, before that. There
had been opportunities. But she had kept putting it off,
waiting for the perfect moment that never came. She had
delayed too long, and the thing everybody kept warning

her about had happened. Somebody else had told him first.

So what? Wasn't he just one more self-centred, conceited male she was well rid of? But Lucy's anger had cooled now and she couldn't whip it up again. Instead, she was remembering all the good things about him. His care and concern for his patients, the way he had wrecked his precious boat without a second thought to give that child the maximum chance of life, the way he had tried to shield her from those reporters. His wit, his humour, his tenderness—the budding love between them. All the good things—and so many more of them, and all the more important than his few faults. . .

Lucy burst into tears and wept as she hadn't wept for years.

# CHAPTER NINE

'MR MARSHALL, multiple fractured ribs,' said Charge Nurse Kynoch as soon as he and Lucy had exchanged good mornings. 'Dr Baird saw him first and seemed to think he'd punctured a lung. That must be why she called Mr Lennox in. Essie Munro tells me he was looking thunderous last night—and no wonder! Dr Baird should have called the registrar, not a consultant.' He nodded towards the viewing screen. 'His films. I don't think there are any more changes for you, Lucy.'

'Thanks, John.' Lucy was glad to turn away and look at those X-rays. She had had a sleepless night and she knew it showed. John Kynoch would have noticed, even if he was too polite to comment. She recorded the number and site of the fractures in her notebook, then looked at the case notes for background data. Poor old dear, she thought. Not a nice thing to happen to a man in his eighties. 'I take it he's had routine pethedine?' she asked without turning round.

'About fifteen minutes since, so he should be ready for you soon.'

'Thanks. How's Peter Niven?'

'That leg's not looking any better, I'm sorry to say. It's a good thing we've got Jim Buchan in the ward.' John Kynoch didn't need to add why.

'Yes, he'll set a good example of coping with a prosthesis.' Except that Mr Buchan had a sedentary job and wasn't athletic. Poor Peter! Now *he* had a real problem. Fairly puts your own into perspective, doesn't it, Lucy Trent? 'I'll get started,' she decided.

Mr Marshall, the new patient, first. Someboy had thoughtfully switched beds around so that he was next to Calum Sinclair who, having suffered the same calamity, could be relied on to provide encouragement. Not unexpectedly, the old man was very distressed, though not quite for the reason Lucy had expected. 'They'll not let me get up, lass, and I have tae collect ma pension the day.'

'You'll not be needing any money in here, Mr Marshall,' Lucy soothed him. 'The main thing is to get your chest right.'

'Ach, it's only a wee bit bruising, hen. Nothing much. But I havenae paid ma papers. Nor the milk. . .'

'I'm noting it all down, Mr Marshall, and somebody will take care of all that for you.'

'Tell Willie,' said Mr Marshall. His son, who had been driving the car and was able to go home after treatment.

'I'll do that—and I'm sure he'll be only too pleased to attend to your bits of business.' A fruity cough from the patient intervened and Lucy said, 'It seems to me you could use some help from me too. Now then, here's what we'll do. . .'

'Fair put one to shame, the old yins, do they not?' asked Calum Sinclair when Lucy had cleared the old man's chest of sputum withut the least complaint from the patient. 'You and I ken fine how yon ribs must be paining him, yet all he's bothered about is paying his bills.'

'Remember that pain is a different thing to different people,' Lucy pointed out.

'And that doesnae make me feel any better—remembering the fuss I made!' retorted the patient humorously.

'But you had broken ribs on both sides—and your dislocated hip to contend with as well.'

'And you're a very kind wee lassie to say so.'

'I'm glad you said that, because now you'll understand when I give you a heavier weight to lift today.'

'I should a' kept ma big mouth shut,' he groaned.

The class passed off with the usual good-natured teasing from the patients, though Lucy's replies were less witty than usual. 'Ye're not still worrying about what that bluidy rag the *Clarion* said, are ye, ma lass?' wondered Mr Buchan as she fixed him up with the slings and springs he needed for his special exercises.

She conjured up a smile. 'Not really, Mr Buchan. With young Gavin recovered and going home tomorrow, they've probably lost interest.'

'Aye, and with a bit o' luck, some other disaster'll take their attention in time for the weekend.'

Lucy thanked him for the kind thought, while hoping relief would not be won in quite the way he had suggested.

Of course Kevin couldn't let her lacklustre appearance pass without comment. 'You and the boyfriend had a row, then, Lucy?' he wanted to know.

Lucy fixed him with a steady look. 'You weren't feeling too good on Tuesday; now it's my turn to feel one degree under, that's all,' she retorted.

'Lucy's got a hangover. Lucy's got a hangover,' he chanted. Yes, you had to hand it to him—he never missed a trick. What a pity those quick wits couldn't be put to better use than getting drunk and careering round the city on a motorbike. Perhaps the medical social worker would manage to fix him up with some job training, once his femur was healed. . .

Peter Niven had been very quiet all morning, but whether from pain or depression, Lucy couldn't be sure. She went through his limited exercise routine with him and decided not to comment. Sometimes it was kinder not to; the trick lay in knowing how to react. She hoped she'd got it right. 'Anything I can get for you before I go, Mr Niven?' she asked gently, but he merely shook his head, eyes closed, for answer.

A long walk and a flight of stairs for Mike Craig, who now needed restraining, rather than urging, and the morning ended with another visit to Mr Marshall. Lucy hadn't seen Iain, or indeed any of the doctors, but as this was Thursday—planned ops day—that wasn't surprising.

'Lucy!' She had been passing the door of the treatment-room and the piercing whisper from within startled her. She stopped and looked round to see Essie in the doorway. Essie was wearing a plastic apron and the room was a shambles. 'It'll only take me two minutes to tidy this place up,' she said with unusual optimism, 'and then I'll chum you down to the canteen. Come in and shut the door.' Lucy obeyed, and Essie charged on with, 'You're a little dark horse, are you not, then, Miss Lucy Fearnan Trent? But never mind that now. I've got something to tell you that I think you'd better know. I was on late duty yesterday.'

'Oh, yes,' put in Lucy, pretty sure of what was coming. She gathered up used swabs and other debris and swept it all into the rubbish bin. Better to be busy. . .

'And what with one thing and another, I was very late going off duty,' continued Essie as if Lucy hadn't interrupted. 'Then when I was whizzing through Outpatients on my way out, I heard voices coming from Iain Lennox's room, so naturally I slowed down. "Are you sure?" I heard him ask, sounding absolutely staggered, and then Lois Baird said, "Positive. I got it from Dr Crawford who also lives in those flats. She's Maggie Fearnan's daughter all right. So how would you feel about having Maggie Fearnan for a mother-in-law?" I couldn't make out what he said to that, but it sounded rather as if somebody was trying to strangle him. Then——'

'Did you happen to hear the exact words with which Lois broke the news?' Lucy cut in, desperate to get to the really important bit.

'No, she'd done that before I was near enough.' Essie eyed Lucy sternly. 'You must know fine that he and your mother don't get on, so why ever did you not tell him yourself? It was the sensible thing to do.'

'Do you think I don't realise that?' asked Lucy miserably. 'I wanted to, only—only——' She gulped.

Essie put her strong bowling arm round her shoulders and gave her a cracking squeeze. 'There, there—I'm sure you'll soon manage to smooth him down. Especially now you're forewarned.' Oh, Essie! It's already too late, if you only knew! thought Lucy. But Essie hadn't finished yet. 'He'll never believe all that stuff about it being a put-up job to make him a laughing stock—to get even for whatever it's supposed to be,' she wound up, seizing a cloth wrung out in Savlon and sloshing energetically at all the table-tops.

Lucy stared, gulped again and pounced. 'What stuff? Tell me quickly, Essie—please!'

'As I told you, I didn't hear what she said at first, but as they went on it seemed to me that she must have told him that you and your mother had hatched a plot to get him interested in you. And then when he was—just to dump him. Not that I'd condemn you if you had,' added Essie, hedging her bets. 'Some men are a sight too cocky for their own good—and ours.'

'Good God, Essie, I'd never do a thing like that—never! But, guessing that Iain would be interviewing me in Tom's absence, and knowing how much Iain dislikes her, Ma thought it'd be sensible if I didn't mention her, in case it scuppered my chances. Once I'd got the job, the idea was to let it sort of leak out, once I'd proved myself professionally. Neither my mother nor I dreamed that things would—would take off the way they did.'

'There you are, then,' said Essie. 'Tell him that the way you've just told me and you've not got a thing to worry about.'

If only it were that easy! Essie, of course, had no idea how far things had gone between her and Iain, and Lucy shrank from telling her about last night's stormy and destructive scene. Now she could see exactly why Lois had called Iain in so unnecessarily last night. It was worth risking his displeasure about that, to get her spiteful version told before things went any further—especially if she knew, or suspected, that Lucy was actually in his flat!

'Shove over,' said Essie. She had finished the tables and was now attacking the floor with a mop. Lucy stepped aside obediently.

The floor done, Essie peeled off her apron and washed her hands. 'Good! Now we can go to lunch.'

'Thanks, Essie, but I—I don't feel like eating.'

Essie faced her friend, hands on hips. 'Are you going to give Lois Baird the chance of saying that you're ashamed to appear in public?'

There was only one possible response to that. 'You're quite right, Essie—I never thought of that. So if you're ready, then let's go.'

'Good girl, but scrub your hands first. I saw you helping me to clear up.'

'Yes, Staff Nurse.' Lucy went meekly to the washbasin.

'Save the shy, retiring maiden act for Iain Lennox,' Essie advised. 'Something tells me he'll not be able to resist it.'

'Too late,' admitted Lucy heavily. 'He's called me a feminist more than once—just in fun—but thanks to Lois he probably believes it now.'

'Perhaps you'll feel more cheerful when you've had something to eat,' sighed Essie, sounding quite depressed herself.

Her hope wasn't to be realised. The sight of Iain sharing a quiet lunch with Lois before the afternoon theatre session started Lucy on her own afternoon feeling gloomier than ever.

Like Mr Buchan in the morning, Sally Lawson thought Lucy was still worrying about the *Clarion's* scurrilous report. Lucy didn't deny it. Anything was better than having Sally guess the truth.

The old ladies were less perceptive, being more concerned with their own problems. Trisha was too, having quarrelled with Kevin the day before. For Lucy, the afternoon seemed unending.

John Kynoch had gone off duty and it was Sister Clyde who sat behind the office desk when Lucy was free at last to look in and say she was leaving.

'Somebody will be coming to treat Mr Marshall again this evening, I hope.'

'Yes, Sister. Mrs Lawson is on tonight.'

'Good.' Sister rose from her desk and switched on the kettle. 'I always have tea about now, work permitting, and I'm sure you could do with a cup before you go, Lucy.'

'Thank you, Sister—that's very kind of you,' accepted Lucy, advancing into the room. She might be anxious to get away before Iain came to look at his afternoon op patients, but she couldn't overlook Sister's kind offer.

Iain came before the tea was brewed, and with him came Lois, fussing and twittering. 'No, no, you take the chair, Iain—I'll be fine on the windowsill.'

She's behaving more like a nannie or an anxious wife than a house officer, thought Lucy, trapped in her corner by the new arrivals. Sister cut through Lois's manoeuvrings by asking, 'Is your bleeper not working, then, Dr Baird?' Lois looked blank. 'Mr Murray has been trying to find you this last half-hour. He wants you down in A and E.'

Lois frowned and muttered that she was off at six, while Iain advised, 'Better hurry, Lois. You know Charles hates to be kept waiting.'

There was no arguing with him, but before she went, Lois opened her blue eyes very wide and cooed, 'I'll try not to be late tonight, Iain.'

Guess who that's really aimed at, thought Lucy—though not without a pang, as Iain replied calmly, 'If you are, it can't be helped. Work comes first.'

There then ensued a discussion on the management of today's ops cases between Sister and Iain, in which Lucy took no part. She just sat there, sipping her tea and watching him; miserably aware that tonight was the night she would have cooked dinner for him, but for Lois's spiteful intervention. Now, instead, it was Lois with whom he meant to spend the evening. Inevitable that he should turn to her again, so why had she not expected that?

Lucy noted the proud tilt of his head, the intelligent gleam of professional zeal in the tawny eyes as he debated with Sister. Picking up a pencil, he drew a few swift, skilful strokes on the memo pad, the better to indicate the exact method he had used. 'Now if only I had the X-rays——'

'I'll fetch them,' said Sister quickly, rising to her feet before he could.

When she had gone, Iain folded his arms across his chest and stared fixedly at the wall, avoiding Lucy's unhappy stare. I can't stand this, she thought miserably. Another long second or two of tense silence and she had blurted out, 'I lost my temper last night.'

Iain's gaze didn't shift from that blank wall as he returned a curt, 'Yes.'

'I wish I hadn't, but I was so anxious—worried. . .'

Now he did look at her, and his eyes were dark and cold and distant. 'It's a normal reaction to bluster and shout when defending the indefensible.'

'Now look here——!' she burst out furiously.

'You're doing it again,' he said, just as Sister returned.

Lucy gasped, gulped and scrambled to her feet. 'Thank you very much for the tea, Sister. Such a—a nice ending to the day. . .'

What a fatuous exit line! About as fatuous as that attempt at an apology. Now she'd made things even worse. Yet how could a girl with any spirit be expected to keep her temper when she saw something potentially so precious slipping away from her? Wasn't it only natural to fight?

Fight, yes—but only if one could keep a cool head. I'll write to him, decided Lucy, as she gained the haven of the empty changing-room. I'll set it all down exactly as it was—as I told it to Essie. Surely he'll come round then—if he feels anything at all for me, that is. In any case, I've nothing to lose by trying.

In order to get to her car, she had to pass through the consultants' car park. Iain's sleek black Audi was there—and he was sitting behind the wheel. Just about to drive off home to get ready for his evening with that snake-in-the-grass Lois! Lucy forgot her decision to write and once more yielded to instinct. Almost before she knew it, she was beside the car and bending to the open window. 'Iain, please listen to me!'

His right arm rested on the door frame and only the

restless drumming of his fingers betrayed his awareness of her presence. 'I was—quite sincere, Iain. Truly I was,' she assured him.

Without looking at her he said, 'I'd be more inclined to believe that if you'd been honest with me from the first.'

'It was—difficult. I needed to choose my moment. And anyway, I wasn't concealing anything very dreadful. If I'd had a string of lovers—or children—or had been to gaol. . . Oh, why can't you understand that I——?'

He turned his head and regarded her with a cool and steady calm. 'And why can you not understand that this is *finis*? Deceit apart, you're just not the girl I thought you were. To be blunt, you're a disappointment. It's as simple as that.' He looked past her, his attention taken by the sound of high heels pattering eagerly across the tarmac. 'I think it would be better if you went—now.' Lucy was dismissed.

What could she do but obey? She turned away, stumbling blindly towards her own car, which she unlocked with fingers that trembled. Clumsily she dropped into the driving seat. It was long after Iain had driven past with Lois preening beside him that Lucy felt capable of driving away herself.

Unable to face a long and lonely evening in the flat, she headed south-west towards Pollok Park. She left the car and wandered the winding gravel paths, oblivious of others passing. She had miscalculated completely back there and had made an utter fool of herself. Far from falling in love, Iain had been cynically looking her over; assessing her worthiness to be next in a long line of girlfriends. And his interest, shallow and selfish as it was, had not survived the discovery that she was the daughter of that redoubtable surgeon Maggie Fearnan—

whose only crime was that she had, more than once, got the better of him!

Essie, that no-nonsense girl, thought him a chauvinist. Tom, calm and wise, considered him too attractive for his own good. She'd have been better to heed their objective opinions than to rely on her own reading of him—based as it was on nothing more reliable than wishful thinking!

Well, she wasn't the first woman to be so deluded, and she wouldn't be the last. Not that that was much comfort. God, was there ever such a fool?

Lucy emerged from the trees beside a field, where a police dog training exercise was keeping a large crowd entertained. Having nothing better to do, she watched too. But as the shadows lengthened, she realised that she was hungry. The restaurant in the Burrell Gallery would have closed long since, so slowly, unwillingly, Lucy returned to her car.

On reaching home, she went straight to the kitchen to make coffee and a sandwich. While she was taking her third bite, the phone rang. Absurd to be so disturbed—it would be anybody in the whole world but he.

'Lucy? I've been trying to get you all evening,' said a man whose voice she didn't recognise, until he went on, 'Young Gavin's being discharged tomorrow, and I thought it'd be a nice angle if you could be there for a shot or two.'

Of course—Simon Mackie, the TV producer. 'That would depend on the time of day,' Lucy told him.

'Around lunchtime, they said.'

'That might just be possible.' And very possibly an annoyance to Iain Lennox?

'Great! So how about meeting for a drink to discuss it?'

'You mean—now?' she asked.

'Sure. There's rather a nice wee wine bar round the corner from your place. Say—ten minutes?'

'Splendid. I could do with a good stiff drink,' said Lucy.

# CHAPTER TEN

LUCY approached the wards that Monday morning at nothing like her usual brisk pace. On the half landing of the stairs, she paused, yawning and gazing unseeingly out of the window. She had been on duty and very busy all weekend. Last night she had had less than three hours' sleep between visits to the Intensive Care Unit. She yawned again. Today was going to be very difficult— and not only because she was so tired. Today Iain would be back.

The week following their quarrel had been unpleasant, to say the least. He had avoided her as much as possible, conveying messages through third parties. This caused much whispering and speculation among both staff and patients, and all the time there was Lois—triumphant, and ever ready with some barbed remark. Iain's departure for a Hebridean sailing holiday had been a positive relief—even if Lois had also been away for part of that time. Because Lois had left nobody in any doubt that she was going sailing too.

The only small plus in Lucy's life had been Simon Mackie. Her brief TV appearance with wee Gavin McCluskey outside the Northern General Hospital on the day of his discharge had closed the chapter of the rescue and the short-lived notoriety that went with it. By way of reward for her co-operation, Simon had taken Lucy for a Chinese meal. He had been cheerful and amusing, and when he asked her out again, she went. And why not?

But now, three weeks on, Simon was making it very

clear that he was looking for more than company and conversation. So Lucy had another problem. She sighed and yawned again.

Brisk firm steps in the corridor below, along with the tip-tap of spiky heels, galvanised Lucy into action. She took the remaining stairs two at a time and when Lois and Iain entered the office minutes later she was looking as if she'd been there for ages. Pen poised over notebook, she was listening to Sister's Monday morning update. The perfect picture of the perfect physio. Well, nearly. It was yet another yawn that spoiled the effect.

'I hope you had a pleasant weekend, Miss Trent,' Iain observed satirically.

Lucy regarded him, wide-eyed and wounded. Yet it was a step forward that he had spoken to her at all. 'I've had a very busy weekend on duty, Mr Lennox,' she answered with quiet dignity. The briefest of pauses and then, 'I hope you and Dr Baird have had a pleasant holiday. You certainly had marvellous weather.' Nobody could accuse her of harbouring a grudge!

'I can't answer for Dr Baird, but I certainly have,' Iain returned calmly.

Had Lois's tale of sailing been nothing but a fairy story, then? But Lucy had to believe him, with his clear eyes and enhanced tan, as he continued, 'We'd like to do a quick round to fill in the gaps—if you have the time, Sister.'

'I anticipated that, Mr Lennox, and everything is ready.' Sister smiled at Lucy. 'There are still one or two other points, dear, but they'll keep for the moment.'

'Thank you, Sister.'

As Lucy turned to go, Lois tinkled, 'Oh, Iain, I'm so sorry, but I can't possibly come round just now. I've got to take the blood samples before the lab collection.'

'You didn't think of coming to the wards earlier than

usual in order to have time for both?' Iain asked with only a minimal trace of impatience.

'No, I didn't know you'd want to do a round.'

'I see.' Impossible to tell from his tone what exactly it was he was claiming to see, but Lucy went off frowning all the same. She could well imagine the blasting anybody but his girlfriend would have got for such lack of foresight! A thought that served to underline what Lucy had already accepted. She had been nothing but a slight hiccup in his relationship with that dozy blonde. Well, Lois was welcome to him! What girl in her right mind would want a man that selfish and choosy and fickle?

'We're surely in for it the day, guys,' observed Kevin sagely after one look at Lucy's stern expression.

'You can count on it,' she promised. 'But not quite yet. There's to be an extra ward round, so the class will have to wait.'

Iain would find a lot of changes. Of the patients in this ward when he went away, only five remained; three fractured femurs on traction, Calum Sinclair—still on traction for that damaged hip, and Peter Niven.

Lucy went to Peter first. By some miracle, the collateral circulation Iain had managed to establish to Peter's mangled right leg had held, but it was going to be a long, hard job restoring function. Not for the first time Peter asked now, 'Would it not have been quicker if I'd just had the leg off and got an aritifical one, Miss Trent?'

As always before, Lucy agreed, 'Yes, much quicker.' A pause. 'But you've got to take the long-term view. Surely it's better to spend a year or so getting that leg back into shape, rather than the next sixty years or more doing without it?'

He smiled crookedly. 'You think I'll live that long?'

'Why ever not? You're a fine specimen of a man—

apart from a few temporary problems with arms and legs, that is.'

'Is that all I've got, then? You sure know how to cheer a man up, Miss Trent!'

'All part of the service,' Lucy smiled. 'Now then, I'm going to do the lanolin massage to your skin grafts first. OK?'

Some time later, the cubicle curtains were drawn aside and Iain looked down at the work in progress. 'Those grafts look very healthy and mobile, Miss Trent.'

'Yes, they are, sir.'

Iain exchanged a few words with the patient before telling him, 'You're doing very well, lad.'

'Then it's thanks to you, sir—and Miss Trent here.'

'Quite so. Surgery alone seldom succeeds without good physiotherapy to follow.' A brief approving nod which might have been for either or both of them and Iain withdrew. Had he decided to move on from cold war to careful neutrality, then? Only time would tell. All the same, it was a possibility that Lucy found cheering.

In the canteen, Essie and Lucy had paid for their lunches and were making for the nearest empty table. 'Anyway, so what?' asked Essie, resuming the monologue she'd been giving all the way here. 'Holiday or no holiday, she'll not last any longer than the others, you mark my words. That man's a—a desert sheikh at heart!'

Lucy sighed inwardly. Sometimes she wished Essie would show her friendship in some other way than by constantly running Iain down. It hurt. It shouldn't, but it did. 'He's bound to settle down some time,' she supposed. 'So why not now? And it'd be sensible to marry a doctor. Shared interests and all that.'

'Rubbish,' retorted Essie crisply. 'That didn't work for your parents, did it?'

There was no answer to that, other than the obvious. Lucy picked up her fork and twisted it round and round in a plate of spaghetti that didn't smell very nice. What in the world had prompted her to choose such a thing anyway on such a hot and sticky day? She stood up. 'I'm taking this back and having a sandwich instead,' she told Essie.

Returning minutes later, Lucy halted uncertainly on seeing Charles sitting down beside Essie, while Iain took the vacant chair opposite. 'Yes, it is crowded today, isn't it?' Essie was saying. 'It's all the folk on the special course they're running for administrators.'

'You mean they actually teach them how to truss up us poor workers in all that red tape?' Iain asked humorously, a further quip dying on his lips at sight of Lucy.

'I—er——' she stammered helplessly, looking round in vain for another seat.

'Your seat, I believe,' Iain said gruffly, pulling in his chair to let her get by.

He knew that and had still accepted Essie's offer. Or had that been Charles's doing? Hardly a matter of choice, though, with the place so crowded.

'I'm very glad to see you, Lucy,' said Charles. 'You see, something very important has cropped up for tonight and I've had to cry off the skittles match. Could you possibly stand in for me?'

Ten out of ten for tactlessness, thought Lucy, glad to be able to say, 'Sorry, Charles, but I've got a date too.'

She sensed Iain stiffening as he remarked, 'After such a busy weekend? I'm surprised you've got the stamina.'

'My friend is very understanding,' Lucy returned quietly—and quite untruthfully. Because, on present showing, understanding was something that Simon was not.

'Then why not bring him too?' suggested Essie wickedly. 'We really need you, Lucy.'

'Not from what I've seen of your play—and Mr Lennox's.' Oh, thank you, Essie, for making sure he knows my anonymous friend is a man!

Essie and Charles continued trying to persuade her, but Lucy wasn't for moving. 'And now if you'll excuse me, I have to go. Good luck for tonight,' she added graciously, to show how well brought up she'd been.

Iain answered that with a veritable snarl of derision. Why? It couldn't matter that much to him as long as his precious Lois was playing.

About halfway through the afternoon, when Lucy and Sally were teaching the use of elbow crutches to a patient who just couldn't get the hang of it, Iain appeared in the ward and stood there, watching them and making them all three nervous. Realising this, he walked away and stood with his back to them, talking to Trisha. 'I'm waitin' for my turn at the dancin',' they heard her say.

'What did you make of that lady, Miss Trent?' asked Iain when the patient had been returned to her chair.

'I think she must have some pro-prioceptive loss, sir. She doesn't seem to have a clue about placing either her feet or her crutches.'

Iain nodded his agreement. 'I came to that conclusion when I examined her this morning, so I've asked one of the neurologists to look her over.'

'Yes, sir.' When he didn't walk away, Lucy said tentatively, 'Is it all right if we walk Trisha now?'

'Please—go ahead.' He continued to hover, and afterwards, when Sally went off to start her individual treatments, he signed for Lucy to stay. 'Have you heard how Mr Buchan is getting on as an outpatient?' he asked.

'I'm told he's managing his prosthesis very well and only needs one stick for balance.'

'Splendid. And Bob Walker?'

'He can flex that knee to a right angle and is building up good muscle bulk.'

'Splendid,' he repeated, going on to require details of the progress of every other patient discharged in his absence and now attending for outpatient treatment. 'I hope I haven't taken up too much of your time,' he said at last, quite courteously.

'Not at all—I quite understand,' returned Lucy, while not at all sure that she did. If he was that anxious for an update, wouldn't it have been better to go down to Physio and question those therapists currently treating his patients? But perhaps he didn't want to leave the wards. Certainly he was much in evidence for the rest of the afternoon.

And still there at five-thirty when Lucy went to tell Sister Clyde that she was going off duty now. 'And about time too, dear—you look as if you're just about asleep on your feet. I think you should have a nice relaxing bath as soon as you get home, and then get to bed early.'

'Sister is giving you some very good advice,' seconded Iain, picking up the phone as it started to ring.

He listened for a second or two, frowning heavily before saying, 'You may speak to her on this occasion, but please keep it brief. Hospital lines are not intended for personal calls.' He handed the receiver to Lucy, saying coldly, 'For you.'

He was looking so fierce that Lucy had quite decided it must be Maggie calling, but it was only Simon to say how sorry he was, but he'd have to cancel their date. 'That's all right, Simon—not to worry,' Lucy answered quickly. She would have put down the phone, but he insisted on giving his reasons in detail. 'Simon, it's all right—I quite understand,' she managed to interject as she encountered Iain's stony stare. 'Look, I've got to go—I think one of the surgeons wants to use the phone. See you.'

Meanwhile, Sister had gone to fill her kettle for the ritual tea and they were alone. 'Stood you up, has he?' asked Iain provokingly.

'Not exactly. There's a bit of a crisis in the newsroom, so he can't get away, that's all.'

'Then you can stand in for Charles after all.'

'I couldn't possibly do that,' said Lucy. 'Sister advised me to get an early night and you backed her up, remember? So I'm going to obey both of you.' As she left the room, she heard Iain draw in his breath on a loud hiss.

Next morning Iain was parking his car as Lucy passed through the area reserved for the consultants. She averted her eyes and headed fast for the entrance, but with his long easy stride, he caught up with her in time to hold open the heavy swing door. Lucy murmured thanks and Iain asked abruptly, 'Are you feeling less tired today?'

Kind of him—if he hadn't sounded more censorious than concerned. Lucy raised her head just that little bit higher. 'Thank you—yes, I am.' Several yards were covered in an uneasy silence before she thought of asking, 'How did the skittles match go?'

'We lost.'

'Oh, dear—I wouldn't have thought that possible with Essie on the team.'

'Last night Essie's mind was anywhere but on the job,' Iain said stiffly.

'Really?' Lucy slowed down as they neared Physiotherapy. 'This is where I. . .'

'Quite.' Iain stalked on towards Outpatients and his consulting-room. Lucy stared after him, trying to guess at his thoughts. Then with a puzzled shake of the head, she went to change into uniform.

Essie was off that morning, but when Lucy returned to the unit after lunch, Essie poked her head out of the office and called, 'Lucy, could I speak to you, please? It's urgent.'

'I'll go on and get started,' said Sally as Essie hauled Lucy into the office.

She shut the door and leaned against it. 'You're not to laugh,' she ordered. 'Promise!'

'Promise,' said Lucy, totally mystified. She'd been expecting to hear something about a patient.

At that Essie turned the colour of beetroot and said self-conciously, 'I'm—getting married.'

'Essie, that's wonderful! Oh, I'm so pleased for you. But why on earth did you think I might laugh?'

'We-ell, I'm not exactly a candidate for Miss World, am I?'

'Good grief, Essie, how many of us are? And you must know what lovely eyes you've got. Who's the lucky man?'

Essie was marrying a minister—a lifelong chum from schooldays. Cupid had fired his first dart last Saturday at a conference of Christian Youth, and this morning, over coffee in Fraser's, Alan had proposed, taking them both completely by surprise. 'He says he doesn't know what came over him—and neither do I,' Essie added drolly.

'No? Well, I bet I do—you probably took off those horrible glasses,' Lucy divined confidently.

'Do you know, I believe I did?' Essie realised.

'So now you've absolutely got to get some with pretty frames,' Lucy ordered. 'But come on—I want all the details!'

Essie was only too happy to reveal all, and they were

happily debating traditional white versus something sensible that would come in useful afterwards, when the door swung open and Iain came in with Lois. Essie only just had time to swear Lucy to secrecy with a finger to her lips.

At sight of those two faces, Lucy temporarily forgot Essie's exciting news. Lois was looking triumphant, while Iain looked as if he'd just been poleaxed. What on earth could have happened? Don't say he had got carried away like Essie's Alan and proposed to Lois?

Such a thought was too painful to be borne. Hurriedly Lucy said, 'Thanks for giving me so much of your time, Staff,' winked at Essie—proud of her red herring—and escaped.

In the women's ward, Sally brushed aside Lucy's apology and said hesitantly, 'I hate having to ask this so soon after your hectic weekend, but I've tried everybody else——' She broke off, biting her lip.

Lucy had already guessed what was coming. 'All right, out with it,' she said resignedly.

'Craig rang up. His boss has asked us to dinner tonight—almost a Royal command! It's only to make up numbers, we gather, but all the same, if we go—and make a good impression—it could help Craig's career. But I'm on call. . .' Sally looked as if she might burst into tears.

Lucy stifled a small sigh and said, 'Not to worry—I'll do it.'

'You will? Oh, Lucy what a pal you are! Now I simply must find a phone——' Sally dashed away, transformed from gloom to glee in an instant. Lucy started work, thinking, all this joy about. I wish a little bit of it would come my way.

The afternoon passed without incident and, unlike

yesterday's, without Iain hovering constantly on the sidelines.

As the girls returned to Physio, Sally asked belatedly, 'Are you sure it's all right about tonight, Lucy?'

'Positive. I wasn't doing anything anyway.'

'You are good.'

'Yes, I am, aren't I? It quite overwhelms me sometimes.'

'And so witty too!'

'That as well. In fact, I'm just too marvellous altogether. So why don't more people notice?' Seriously Lucy said, 'I do hope things will go well for you tonight, Sally.'

Ringing home soon afterwards, Lucy left a message on the answering machine, telling her mother that she'd not be there to cook supper after all. Then she went to join the queue for the shower.

One o'clock in the morning. Lucy was struggling out of a troubled dream. That shrill ringing was not, after all, church bells at the Iain/Lois wedding, but the telephone beside the bed. Quite disorientated, she felt around in the dark. She found it and asked sleepily, 'Yes, who is it?'

'Paediatrics. Can you come at once, please?' That had sounded very urgent.

'Sure.' An instinctive response to any nocturnal summons, but as yet Lucy wasn't even sure where she was. Switching on the light, she recognised with surprise the tiny room in Physio, kept for just such busy nights. She got out of bed and into uniform. She must have been deeply asleep. Normally she only cat-napped on duty nights, but she'd been so tired—and so depressed. . .

A splash of ice-cold water to the face helped to bring her round.

The patient was a tiny baby with unseasonal bronchiolitis, newly admitted and in some respiratory distress. With the baby laid carefully across Lucy's knee, five minutes of gentle vibrations and suction was enough to unclog the tiny chest, bringing relief to both the baby and her frantic mother.

The crisis over, Lucy looked at her watch. She was due in ICU again in half an hour, which meant there was no point in returning to Physio. So what to do meantime? Her own unit was right next door, and with John Kynoch now on nights, there was every chance of a hot, strong, reviving coffee. Lucy was very glad she had remembered that.

On stepping into the main corridor of Orthopaedics, she was astounded to hear a loud crash and frightened cries coming from the isolation ward nearby. She reached the door in one bound and, pushing it wide, she saw a man staggering about brandishing a knife, while blood spurted in great fountains from his wrists. Lois, shaking violently, was cowering in a corner with her hands over her face.

The adrenalin flowing fast, Lucy launched herself at the man with all her strength. The knife dropped from his grasp and he fell across the bed. Hitting the alarm button—giving Lois a calming slap—issuing some very crisp instructions. By the time John Kynoch came running with two nurses at his heels, the patient was lying quietly on his back with his arms pointing skywards and makeshift pads pressed and held firmly over his slashed arteries.

One glance sufficed for John to grasp the situation— and who had coped. 'Well done, Lucy. We'll take over now.'

Lucy walked round the bed and, taking Lois by the

arm, she led her away to the office, where she thrust her into a chair. Lois slumped there, silent.

The kettle was hot and boiled in seconds. Lucy made two mugs of instant coffee and handed one to Lois.

Lois peered at it and said plaintively, 'I don't like it black.'

'Hard luck—there isn't any milk.'

They drank in a silence which Lucy felt no inclination to break. She was too tired, too weary, and also full of disgust at Lois's craven behaviour. A chance glance at the clock reminded her it was time to move on, and she got up to leave.

'L-Lucy?' It was a strangled whisper.

'What?'

'Y-you'll not tell, will you? How I—I panicked, I mean. If that should get out. . .' Lois's eyes were wide with desperate appeal.

'There's no need for me to tell, is there?' said Lucy coldly. 'You'll be doing that yourself.'

Lois looked terrified at that. 'Oh, no—no, I couldn't! I couldn't—and you can't make me!'

'You're a doctor—a doctor who failed in a crisis,' Lucy returned inexorably. 'If I were you, I don't know how I could conceal that, and keep my self-respect. But don't worry. Tale-bearing is not my line—I leave that to people like you!' With that thrust, Lucy left her. Her head was throbbing with fatigue and nervous reaction. But there were four seriously ill patients awaiting her attention. This was no time to be thinking of self.

On the way out, she passed the Charge Nurse and one of the surgical registrars outside Isolation. 'Hang on, Lucy, I need to know what happened,' said John.

'Sorry, John, I'm overdue in ICU, but I'll come back the minute I've finished there. You know how it is.'

Lucy had been referring to the time factor, but John returned grimly, 'Yes, I'm pretty sure I can guess.'

Next morning, Lucy was later than usual going to Ortho, because of the need to report to their regular physios on the overnight condition of the seriously ill patients. She wondered as she went how the inquiry was progressing.

Last night she had given John only the bare facts; hearing the disturbance, going in and applying first aid, with Lois. No mention of Lois's panicky collapse, though she did admit to being the one to overpower the patient. But John was no fool. Besides, Lois had given herself away by her demeanour. Lucy had steadfastly refused to incriminate the girl and tried to divert John by wondering aloud what could have prompted the patient to slash his wrists.

John had shaken his head at that. 'That's one for the shrinks to find out. He'd been drinking, of course—which is probably why he fell and hit his head on that kerbstone. If Surgical Neurology hadn't been full, he'd not have found his way to us at all. What really worries me is that damned knife. How on earth did he manage to conceal it during the admission procedure? There'll be the devil to pay over this.'

Arriving on the unit, Lucy went straight away to look through the viewing window in the door of Isolation, but the bed was empty.

'Transferred to Psychiatry,' explained Iain, coming up behind her and making her jump as if stung. He gave her time to collect herself before saying kindly, 'He's quite all right this morning—thanks to your timely intervention.'

'I just happened to be passing—on the scrounge for a coffee, actually——'

'Come into the office, please, Lucy,' he cut in with

quiet authority. He strode across the corridor, confident
that she would follow. 'Shut the door, please.' Lucy did
so. Iain looked down at her with steady gravity. 'I want
your account of last night's emergency—and in detail.'

Lucy had no means of knowing how much he knew,
or whether he had spoken yet to Lois. After some
thought she said, 'As I've already said, I just happened
to be passing and I heard the sounds of—of a scuffle.
The patient was raving and Dr Baird was—well, she was
in there alone with him. He was bleeding profusely. It
was all a bit hectic, but somehow he was—brought
under control and calmed down, and then we got the
bleeding under control too. Then Mr Kynoch arrived
and took over. That's all, really.'

'Who pressed the alarm button?' asked Iain.

'I did.'

'Because Dr Baird was struggling with the patient?'

'Because I was—nearest.' So she had been.

A spasm of emotion flitted over his face as he persisted,
'And that is really how it was?'

'Yes.'

'There's nothing you wish to add—or change?'

Why? Had Lois been making herself out to be the
heroine of the hour? Unworthy, Lucy. 'Nothing at all,'
she returned quietly.

There was no mistaking the admiration on his face for
any other emotion then. 'Thank you,' he said gratefully.
'I'm quite confident that I can fill in the gaps in your
recollection from other sources.'

Lucy was inclined to think that he knew everything
already. Lois must have owned up, after all. She felt
vaguely ashamed for having doubted her. 'If—if there's
nothing else, then. . .' she began.

'Not for the moment, so you can get back to your

work. There'll be an inquiry, of course. But, Lucy——'
On the point of leaving, she turned quickly. 'Thank you
for keeping such a cool head.'

'Oh, that,' she said. 'That will have been hereditary.
My mother has never been known to fail in a crisis.' She
looked at him steadily, daring him to explode.

He didn't. Instead he answered quietly, 'That is
something I have never had any reason to doubt.' Then
he turned away to answer the clamour of the ever-active
telephone.

# CHAPTER ELEVEN

LUCY sat on a fallen tree stump at the lochside and threw pebbles into the sparkling water. It was Saturday morning and she was bored. Jock was away to Uncle Archie's for his summer fortnight, Netta was on a Saga holiday and Ma—though she was officially off too—had driven down to Glasgow to lecture at a weekend symposium for GPs.

So Lucy was bored. Or rather, boredom was all she was going to admit to. Dwelling on the real, deep-down reason for her listlessness and this horrid leaden feeling in her chest wasn't going to get her anywhere.

Anyway, she'd had the sort of time lately that was quite enough to depress anybody. A truly fearsome working weekend, coming so soon after the break-up with Iain, coping with an attempted suicide in the middle of a heavy night duty and then having—literally—to fight Simon off last Thursday evening. Very undignified, that had been, and not at all what she'd expected of one with his outward suavity. He'd called her frigid and she'd called him an animal. He'd told her she didn't know what she was missing and she'd said she could guess that it wasn't all that much, judging by the way he was going about it.

And then yesterday there had been the inquiry. It had been something of an ordeal, appearing before a panel consisting of the most senior consultants and the unit manager. Everybody connected with the suicide attempt had been interviewed separately. Lucy had stuck to her original version and carefully avoided criticising Lois.

John, on the other hand, had told Lucy that he meant to be absolutely frank. As rumour had it that Lois had come out of her interview in tears, Lucy presumed that the panel had formed a pretty good idea of what had really occurred that night. How the patient happened to have that knife remained a mystery, though the friends who had brought him to the hospital were suspected.

This time Lucy picked up a really big stone and hurled it overarm into the loch. It landed in the water with a satisfying glug. She watched the perfect circles rippling outwards, while she savoured Iain's quiet, stilted, but very sincere congratulations on the way she had handled that poor deranged man. Iain must know exactly what had happened that night, but best not to make too much of his praise. How much of his approval was due to gratitude because she hadn't pointed the finger at his precious Lois?

In the centre of the loch, dozens of little white sails tacked and weaved. A regatta was in progress. Perhaps Iain would have been taking part if *Aurora* had not been wrecked. But no, he couldn't have; he was on duty this weekend. So the cosy cabin in the woods would be empty.

Lucy felt a sudden silly longing to see it again. She resisted the impulse for a while, assembling all sorts of sensible objections. It was a long way—six miles at least. It might not be empty at all; Iain could have lent it to those sailing friends with whom he shared the bigger boat.

On the other hand, she was bored. A walk along the shore to the cabin and back would fill in the time nicely until Ma came home. Lucy ran back to the cottage to change her sandals for walking shoes and put a simple picnic lunch together. Then she set off.

It was a beautiful day, warm and sunny, with just

enough breeze out on the loch to make sailing a pleasure, yet sheltered here at the water's edge, under the over-hanging trees. There was hardly anybody about. People tended to herd together on the beaches near the car parks, in comfortable reach of the snack bars. The woods were vibrant with birdsong, though few of the choristers were showing themselves. A little way from the shore, a raft of ducks argued and paddled.

Lucy plodded on, wishing she'd gone to town with Maggie and put in the day going round the shops, having her hair done—even turning out the flat. None of which would have stopped her thinking, though, any more than this walk was doing. By coming home from London, she had merely exchanged one trough for another. And that was that.

She ate her lunch sitting on a grassy knoll that jutted out into the loch not far from where they had rescued Gavin. Five weeks ago to the day. The deep groove in the beach made by *Aurora's* hull when they ran her ashore was still clearly visible. Hastily Lucy transferred her gaze to a family of swans cruising majestically in line astern near the shore. Perhaps they'd relish her remaining sandwich more than she would. She broke it in pieces and scattered them on the water before moving on.

Several times Lucy had to make a detour inland at points where there was no shore, and again to cross the river at Balloch. It was after three by the time she reached the clearing where the cabin was. Yes, that was the one—set apart from the others, on higher ground and with the best view of the loch. She was unprepared for the wave of emotion that hit her as she drew near. Yet she didn't turn back, but went on until she was no more than ten yards from it. She stared, knowing that until those reporters came, she had been happier in that place than ever in her life before.

The door opened and Iain emerged on the veranda, dressed in the same ancient jeans and tattered shirt he'd been wearing then. He strode to the balustrade, gripping it with both hands and staring in disbelief. 'Lucy?' he asked in a harsh, dry tone.

She took that for a reproof. 'I was out for a walk— and I've come further than I meant to.' As she turned away, she remembered he shouldn't have been there at all.

'Wait!' he called. She halted. 'It was just that I— didn't expect to see you.' She could hear him coming towards her.

'I thought you were on duty,' she said defensively.

'I would have been, only Tom particularly wants next weekend off. So we swapped.'

'Ah.' Lucy couldn't look at him. It was too much just to know he was close without seeing him as well. 'If I hurry, I can just make the bus from Balloch,' she said, knowing nothing about the local transport. She was so vexed at being caught spying, as he must believe.

'Would you like some tea?' Iain asked abruptly, astounding her.

She looked at him then all right, and saw that he was regarding her warily—almost as though he expected her to bite. 'I wouldn't want to trouble you,' she began.

'I wouldn't have offered if I thought you might.'

That was more like the Iain she knew. 'Then thank you very much,' she said, following when he turned away towards the cabin.

Inside, he busied himself in the tiny kitchen putting on the kettle and taking mugs off hooks. 'What's so important as to make Tom change weekends?' wondered Lucy, just for something to say that would break the awkward silence.

'Some relation or other is getting married way up

north next Saturday.' Iain paused. 'There's a lot of it about,' he said deliberately.

Oh, God, he was going to tell her that he was marrying Lois! Swallow hard, keep calm. . . 'Marriage?' she repeated lightly. 'Yes—and why not? Summer's the best time. Come to think of it, I must check the date of my next weekend on for that very reason.' Essie had asked Lucy to be one of her bridesmaids. 'What a good thing I remembered!' Oh, well done, Luce!

Iain had been about to hand her her tea. Instead he put it down heavily on the table, where it slopped over. 'You're pretty cool about it all,' he remarked dully.

Lucy looked at him, mystified by his look which was at once reproving and—sad? 'Do you not feel you could be rushing into this?' he asked hesitantly. 'Marriage is a very serious step.'

'Surely you don't. . .?' But he did, of course. Clear as a recording came the memory of her conversation with Essie the day that Essie told all—and Iain had come in with Lois in the middle of it. He had jumped to the wrong conclusion. And he minded. Yes, he did!

'I agree. Marriage *is* a very serious step. I was just surprised at your thinking I wouldn't think so too, that's all.' Clumsy, but it would buy her time. Time to be sure. . .

Iain thrust his hands in the pockets of his jeans and said truculently, 'But you've only known the man a few weeks!'

'Do you mean Simon?'

He frowned. 'Are you saying there's more than one? Good lord, Lucy, how many men *have* you got on your list?'

'You're not the only one who goes—shopping around,' she returned provocatively.

'And much good it's done me!' He swung round to

stare out of the window, his hands still in his pockets, legs planted firmly apart. But there was a dejected droop to his shoulders. Lucy waited. 'My father never recovered from my mother running off, and I grew up vowing that no woman would ever do that to me.'

'It works both ways,' said Lucy, out of her own experience. 'Men can hurt women just as much as the other way about.'

'I know that—which is why I urge you to think more carefully before you take—that final step.'

'But why?' she asked softly. 'Why should my welfare matter to you?'

'Because I—I. . . We may not exactly hit it off,' he said awkwardly, 'but that's not all your fault. You've got many good qualities. You're a—a very worthwhile person. Dammit, Lucy, can you not just accept that I don't want to see you get hurt?'

'Are you saying that, after all, you—you quite like me?'

'All right, yes—if you want to paraphrase.'

'But you don't like my mother.'

He swung round, frowning. 'What the hell's that got to do with it? I don't like mine either—she's a thorough-going bitch—but we can't help our mothers. And they shouldn't be held against us.'

Now there was a change of tune. 'You say you quite like me, yet it's not very long since you called me scheming and deceitful,' Lucy reminded him.

'And let me remind you that you said some pretty harsh things to me.'

'I was only hitting back because I was hurt. I didn't mean more than about half of it.'

'Half is more than enough. So when's this bloody wedding supposed to be?' he demanded savagely.

'Wedding?' The sudden change of subject had taken

Lucy by surprise. 'The last week in August, I think. Yes, that's right.'

'Let's hope you've worked up a little more enthusiasm by then.'

'I'm enthusiastic now. They're both such dears.' Now he would know he'd jumped to the wrong conclusion, wouldn't he?

Iain stared at her, thunderstruck. 'I don't believe what I'm hearing,' he said dazedly. 'Are you saying you haven't decided yet which one to——You scheming, cold-blooded little——' He fumed helplessly to a standstill.

'Could bridesmaid be the word you're looking for?' suggested Lucy helpfully. 'I'm going to be one of Essie's when she marries her nice Alan next month.'

She had expected relief, if not rapturous delight, when she said that. But all she got was a sort of sober simmering down. Did that mean he was still with Lois after all? She bit her lip and regarded him anxiously.

'So that's the way of it,' he acknowledged. 'Well, I'm glad you're not rushing to the altar.'

Which hadn't answered her unspoken question. 'I'm prepared to believe you mean it kindly,' Lucy said quietly, 'but I really can't see why my personal affairs should be of such interest to you—now.'

'You can't? Then I'll tell you.' He lunged away from her again, to lean his head against the window while he told his story. 'When you flung out of the flat in such a temper after that terrible row, I told myself I was glad. I—liked you. Quite a lot. But enough to stomach Maggie Fearnan as a mother-in-law? Yes, for all my long-held fear of marriage, I'd actually got that length in my thinking,' he underlined, although Lucy hadn't uttered a sound or moved a muscle. 'So I was glad you were out of my life before you came to mean too much to me.

And I went on being glad—for about a week. Then I went away.' He paused.

'My three friends are all happily married, and to very nice women. And as usual the six of them had brought along an unattached girl to even things up. She was very beautiful. Kind as well—and not too talkative either. It was when I found myself quite unable to work up any interest in her that I began to worry.' He laughed—a harsh, brief sound. 'By the end of that fortnight, the poor lass was quite convinced that I was gay!' Another of those mirthless, self-derisory laughs. 'So after all, it was too late. I'd skilfully avoided involvement all those years, only to fall in love without even realising it. I returned to work, determined to get you back. Only to find you apparently planning marriage to somebody else.'

Lucy had crept up behind him during all this. Now she asked wonderingly, 'You mean—you were actually thinking of—of marrying "Battling Maggie Fearnan's daughter"?'

'What I wanted,' Iain said heavily, 'was to marry the one girl without whom life would be empty and utterly meaningless. Unfortunately, she doesn't feel the same. Well, I guess I had it coming.' He heaved himself upright and went to the door. 'So now you know why I—I take such an interest in your welfare.' He opened the door, obviously expecting her to leave—until he saw her face, wet with tears.

'Oh, my darling!' she breathed, thrusting her arms around him and pressing her lips to his.

His response was instantaneous—and would have surprised his erstwhile holiday companion very much indeed.

About an hour later, Lucy raised herself on one elbow and with her free hand, traced the outline of Iain's firm tanned jaw with one tender finger. 'Darling. . .'

'U-um?' He hadn't bothered to open his eyes.

'Maggie will be back at the cottage by now and wondering what's become of her precious daughter.'

Iain opened one eye. 'Think she'll blow a gasket when she finds out?'

'I hope not—and you'd both better behave. I'm not having the two people I love best in all the world at each other's throats.'

Iain groaned. 'You're very like her, you know that?'

'Could be that's why you love me,' teased Lucy, kissing him quickly to prevent an answer, because she hadn't finished yet. 'What I started out to say was how will you feel when it leaks out that you're going to marry Maggie's daughter—after all the things you've said about her?'

This time Iain opened both eyes. 'Like a prize idiot, no doubt, but everything worth having in this life has its price,' he said, pulling her down to underline that with a kiss.

# Three women, three loves . . . Haunted by one dark, forbidden secret.

ALIX ATKINSON

*Boundaries*

*Margaret* – a corner of her heart would always remain Karl's, but now she had to reveal the secrets of their passion which still had the power to haunt and disturb.

*Miriam* – the child of that forbidden love, hurt by her mother's little love for her, had been seduced by Israel's magic and the love of a special man.

*Hannah* – blonde and delicate, was the child of that love and in her blue eyes, Margaret could again see Karl.

It was for the girl's sake that the truth had to be told, for only by confessing the secrets of the past could Margaret give Hannah hope for the future.

## W❂RLDWIDE

# SPARKLING NEW TALENT

Every year we receive over 5,000 manuscripts at Mills & Boon, and from these a few names stand out as the fresh new talent for exciting romantic fiction.

Never before in paperback, we proudly present:

**CHRISTINE GREIG**
A Night-time Affair

**JESSICA HART**
A Sweet Prejudice

**JOANNA NEIL**
Wild Heart

**CATHY WILLIAMS**
A Powerful Attraction

Treat yourself to a feast of love, drama and passion with the best romantic fiction from the best of Mills & Boon's new authors.

**Price: £5.80**
**Published: March 1991**